Then Willie Weaver etches the Crazy Horse Electric game in the mind of every citizen and ball player and coach—maybe every dog and cat—in Coho, Montana. From his unbalanced position, he pivots around on his left leg, *turning his back to the plate,* and *backhands* the ball out of the air. He fields a white-hot, nuclear line drive on pure instinct, robbing Sal Whitworth of a sure triple and Crazy Horse Electric of their fourth straight Eastern Montana American Legion championship. The base runner streaks toward second, his brain several steps behind events. Willie looks into his glove and smiles, waits a split second for his first baseman to catch up, then flips him the ball for the third out.

The crowd sits in stunned silence while the required synapses take place, letting them know what they've just seen really happened, then erupts. The Crazy Horse Electric game is history and Willie Weaver is a minor legend.

CHRIS CRUTCHER is the author of several books for young adults, including *Running Loose* and *Stotan!,* both available in Dell Laurel-Leaf editions. He lives in Spokane, Washington.

ALSO AVAILABLE IN LAUREL-LEAF BOOKS:

The Crazy Horse Electric Game

CHRIS CRUTCHER

LAUREL-LEAF BOOKS

Published by
Bantam Doubleday Dell Books for Young Readers
a division of
Bantam Doubleday Dell Publishing Group, Inc.
1540 Broadway
New York, New York 10036

ISBN: 0-440-20094-6

RL: 7.1

Reprinted by arrangement with Greenwillow Books, a division of
William Morrow & Company, Inc.

Printed in the United States of America

June 1988

OPM   18

For Buddy

— CHAPTER 1 —

Sometimes he remembers it as if it were unfolding in front of him this very minute, all of it; event by amazing event. And sometimes it seems as if it all happened a long, long time ago, maybe in another lifetime. But the focal point, no matter how he thinks about it, is the Crazy Horse Electric game. He still doesn't know if it's the best thing that ever happened to him or the worst thing.

It's two summers ago and sixteen-year-old Willie Weaver walks through the front door of Samson Floral with Petey Shropshire and Jenny Blackburn, the girl Willie would like to be his girlfriend if he could figure out a sure way to make that transformation without destroying their friendship; their history together.

They have a mission.

Mr. Samson is in back, clipping and arranging flowers like he always is. He's seventy-five if he's a day—pretty set in his ways—and Willie knows this won't be easy. The kids stand behind Mr. Samson for a few minutes, watching and clearing their throats and sniffing loudly, in hopes he will notice them, but his hearing aid is dangling from his hip pocket and there's no chance. Finally Willie steps into his field of vision and says, "Hey, Mr. Samson." Mr. Samson jumps, decapitating the begonia he's clipping. He says, "Damn," and replaces the hearing aid in his ear, letting the world back in. "Young Weaver. How are ya, boy?" He swivels on his stool, nodding to Petey and Jenny. "Gonna make my shop famous this year? Win some ball games for Samson Floral?"

"Hope so," Willie says. "Looks like we could have a pretty tough team." He pauses, looking for a better way in to what he wants to say, but Mr. Samson just looks at them all, smiling and nodding slowly. "Actually, that's kind of what we came here to talk to you about . . ."

Mr. Samson's expression is unchanged, his head bouncing gently like that of a plastic beagle with lighted eyes mounted in the rear window of a '57 Chevy.

"Uh, we were wondering if we could talk to you about the caps," Willie says, flinching slightly.

"Of course," Mr. Samson replies. "What's the matter? They too small? Need more caps?"

"No, they fit okay," Willie says, looking to Petey for support. Petey's head hangs; Jenny's hand covers her mouth, stifling a giggle. Willie's on his own. "And there are plenty of them. It's the rose. We took a boatload of crap for the rose last year. We were wondering if maybe we could have a different logo. We'd put 'em on ourselves. I mean, it wouldn't cost anything."

Mr. Samson smiles and turns back to his beheaded begonia; picks it up in a halfhearted attempt to re-attach it to the stem, then lets it fall to the floor. "What did you have in mind?"

Now Petey speaks up. "We were thinking maybe an 'S' over an 'F,' for Samson Floral. You know, like the San Francisco Giants."

Mr. Samson looks over his glasses. "You look at the box scores lately, young fella?"

Petey is blank.

"Giants are dead last. Giants are always dead last." He shakes his head slowly. "Nope. No 'S-F' for us. You boys follow me now. Just follow me out front."

Their eyes roll toward the heavens as they dutifully follow Mr. Samson out onto the sidewalk, where he points to the flashing neon rose above the door. "You kids know how long that sign's been there?"

"Thirty-four years," they say in unison.

"That's the rose on your caps. Identical. You win some games, people see the rose, they make the connection and they buy flowers from me. That's called advertising."

Willie makes a last attempt. "But you have the only floral shop in town. People *have* to buy their flowers from you."

Mr. Samson nods, smiling. "Then the advertising should work," he says. "I think we'll keep the rose." He walks back inside, leaving the kids to stare at the flashing flower and marvel at his logic.

Willie turns to Jenny, who laughs out loud now. "You were a lot of help," he says. "I'll come to *you* first the next time I need backup."

Jenny grins and tweaks his cheek, her long blond single braid whipping behind her head. "I'm with Mr. Samson. I think they're cute. Besides, it makes you work harder to prove yourselves. You know, 'boys named Sue.'"

"Great," Petey says. "Another year of my big brother calling me 'Petunia' every game day. Like it's not hard enough getting any dignity in this world when you're barely five foot three. God, my dad made me wear that stupid cap in our Christmas-card pictures last year."

Willie Weaver walks down the hot, dry two-lane highway with Johnny Rivers—the catcher, not the singer—to practice at Sollie Weaver Field, named after Willie's grandfather, who donated the land and put up most of the money to build it, and who was a legendary athlete around these parts in his day. He played football, basketball and baseball at Notre Dame back before the age of specialization, when an athlete could play as many sports as he was good at. Largely because of Willie, the rose on their caps now has dignity among all teams in the league. Samson Floral is undefeated after ten games.

"It depends on what you can do with Sal Whitworth." Johnny is explaining how Samson Floral can beat Crazy Horse Electric and take the Eastern Montana American Legion Championship away from them. Crazy Horse has won it three years running. "Keep his bat off the ball and we'll own 'em," Johnny says. "They got nobody else can hit you."

"What're you talking about?" Willie says. "They've got hitters clear through the line-up. Jesus, Johnny, their *batboy* hits."

"They can hit," he says, "but they can't hit *you.*"

"They sure hit me last year."

"Last year you were two inches shorter and about thirty pounds lighter and your arm wasn't a licensed nuclear weapon," Johnny says.

Willie smiles. Not even his dad pumps him up the way Johnny does.

"Anyway," Johnny continues, "Whitworth is the key. Blow him over with your fastball and the game is ours." He pauses. "Why don't you just bean him in the first inning? You know, put a hole through his temple; apologize to beat hell, send him a nice card in the neurosurgery ward and we'll win this sucker the easy way."

Willie nods. "Right."

"He won't have to worry about old age that way,"

Johnny says. "Wrinkles. Senility. Uncontrollable bowel movements. Boy, you oughta see my uncle . . ."

They're close to the field now and the rest of the team is waving and hollering at them to hurry up. Petey Shropshire flips a ball into the air with one hand and whacks a high pop fly over the hurricane fence on the right foul line and down the highway toward them. As the ball descends, Willie turns his back, catching it over his shoulder, basket style, like Willie Mays used to do. He flips it to Johnny, who fires it back over the fence.

Willie feels like he can do anything. He's been carrying this team all summer. Samson Floral has some pretty good players, but it doesn't really matter because almost no one in the league can touch Willie's fastball. Over the past twelve months he grew like a weed and though he was expected to trade his quickness and coordination for an involuntary yodel and a forest of zits, it never happened. He just got bigger and stronger and better. He hits from both sides of the plate, thanks to hours of work with his dad—who read that Mickey Mantle's father started working Mick into a switch hitter when he was six—and he throws *heat.*

Willie's mom often tells him he's been given gifts; that he should be thankful for them, but he's not, really. He's always been better at sports than any kid his age, so he's never felt any different than this. It's just the way things are; he's *supposed* to be a hero. He's humble and he seldom brags, but that's mostly because his dad won't have it. Down deep, Willie's a pretty cocky kid; just not cocky enough to mess with William Weaver Sr.

Back then, in those days when Willie was invincible, those days leading up to the Crazy Horse Electric game, his father was mythic to him; and to most other folks in Coho, Montana, too. Big Will played football for the

University of Washington in the early 1960's when the
Huskies beat the Michigan Wolverines 19–6 in the Rose
Bowl; rushed for more than 150 yards and threw a half-
back option touchdown. He was voted Most Valuable
Player. In Coho they had a day in his honor, with a
parade down Main Street and speeches from several
members of the state legislature. It was a big deal. And
when Big Will finally came back to Coho to settle and
raise a family, the town was overjoyed. He was a big
man, over 210, and strikingly good-looking. He kept
himself in excellent physical condition and was always
polite and gracious; always willing to help in that way
small-town people get together to build a garage, or
mow the neighbors' lawn when they're on vacation, or
care for each other's children when parents are ill. As
far back as Willie could remember, folks looked up to
his dad, and the reason it never required a lot of outside
pressure for Willie to do his best was that he wanted
Will Sr. to be proud of him. Yet the two of them were, in
a way Willie never quite understood, somehow distant.
There was a vague, uncomfortable feeling that Big Will
lived through Willie, that Willie's successes were Big
Will's too; and likewise his failures.

Walking with Johnny through the gate, Willie senses
the excitement about the Crazy Horse Electric game.
The chatter is loud and constant; everyone hustles.
Coach Ivy hits flies to the outfielders and Mike Griffith, a
sophomore shortstop at the university, works with the
infield. Second-stringers play catch, throwing each
other high flies and hard grounders.

"You guys are late!" Coach yells. "Where you been?"

"We just got started late," Willie says as Johnny heads
for the dugout to strap on his catching gear. "I thought

my mom was going to bring us, but she didn't come home in time. Sorry."

Coach Ivy lets it go. He runs a fairly loose ship and this isn't important. You don't rattle Tom Seaver before the '69 World Series.

Starters line up in their places; subs move over to the vacant field with Mike Griffith. Johnny crouches behind the plate to catch Willie's warm-ups while Coach Ivy talks about Crazy Horse Electric's hitters, relying on year-old memories and scouting reports because Crazy Horse Electric is from Billings and the two teams have not met this year. Everyone remembers Sal Whitworth, for both his hot bat and his hot head. "All his mistakes last year came from his temper," Coach Ivy reminds them. "Might be a good idea to remember that, Willie."

Willie's arm feels strong and loose. He won't be throwing very hard today because the team needs hitting practice, and because he doesn't want to wear out his arm. He almost wishes the game were sooner because he feels so good, and he fires a couple of hard strikes while Johnny eggs him on. "Heat!" Johnny yells. "That was hot! Gimme another one of those; lemme warm up this ol' mitt. Ooooooh, Willie! Sweet heat!"

Coach Ivy sends a batter up and calls out a situation. "Man on first, one out," and Willie lays one in right down the middle. Johnny's mouth is running loose. "Right down the pipe, big boy. Right down the pipe. Let 'em hit, big Willie; these are the good guys. Only ever played in one game this important," he says, flipping the ball back to Willie, crouching in close to the batter. "Game down in California before I moved up here. Game for the Northern California Babe Ruth League championship . . ."

"He never played for any Northern California championship, Coach," Petey yells in from second base. "This is one of those stupid things he tells. Stop him."

The batter hits a one-hopper to third and Max Craig fields it, fires to Petey on second, who whips around and throws the runner out at first. Double play.

Johnny chatters on. "They had a pitcher, Eric Milfaymee was his name. Big kid. Fast. Almost as fast as our own Dream Weaver. Not quite, but almost. True story."

"Stop him!" Petey yells again.

"We were hitless at the end of the fifth inning and we knew if we didn't do something about this Milfaymee kid we were doomed for sure, so between innings I snuck back and dumped out their water, replaced it with beer; kill some brain cells, slow ol' Eric down a little," Johnny continues, all the while popping the ball into his mitt, then firing it back to Willie, shutting up only long enough for Coach Ivy to call the situation, then forging on with what everyone knows by now will be one of those stupid things Johnny tells.

"It's a hot afternoon and Milfaymee is using up a lot of body fluids, drinking outta that ol' water bucket like there's a big drought comin', but clear through the eighth inning he's still throwin' screamers and we're swingin' at the wind."

"Who wants my allowance?" Petey hollers. "I'll give my allowance to anyone who can stop him." He pauses. "Two weeks' allowance."

Willie's throwing and hitters are hitting and Coach Ivy calls out new situations and none of that slows Johnny down a lick. "But then, in the bottom of the ninth, with the score 0–0, the sun and the alcohol kick in and ol' Milfaymee starts to lose it; walks two batters, then a third. He stops to go take a drink and his coach tries to calm him down. Coach has gotta wanna pull him, but he's got nobody to replace him with.

"So Milfaymee takes a hairy ol' drink and staggers back out to the mound and by now he's seein' double. And he's mad. I'm the hitter an' I'm just lookin' to keep my head. Milfaymee rears back and throws four straight balls—one of 'em hits the backstop eight feet above the plate—and he walks in the winning run."

"Here it comes," Petey yells. "If he does it, let's get him! We'll give you one last chance to stop, Rivers. Oh, God, I'm gonna throw up."

Johnny pops a pitch into his mitt and stands up; raises his catcher's mask to the top of his head and walks out in front of the plate. "Yup," he says, "that was quite a game. Almost as important as this Crazy Horse game coming up."

That's Willie's cue. "The beer, Johnny. Tell us about the beer."

"Ah, the beer," Johnny says, shaking his head as he underhands the ball to Willie. "We called that the beer that made Milfaymee walk us," and he heads for the open field as fast as his stumpy legs will carry him.

"Get him!" Petey screams. "Get him and rip out his tongue!"

Willie flips his glove onto the ground, sits down on the mound and watches as all seven of the others gain on Johnny, who circles around and heads for the backstop, leaps for the center frame support and pulls himself out of Eddie Single's reach by a fraction of a second. He stands on the bar, clinging to the wire mesh behind him, moving laterally back and forth to stomp on the fingers of anyone trying to climb up.

"You guys know about William Tell and his kid when they tried to join the father-son bowling league?"

"Get him!" Petey yells. "Tear down the backstop."

"Computer made a mistake. Somehow it placed their names on three different team rosters."

Petey heads for the water hose; Johnny quickens the story's pace. "The officials at the alley checked the rosters over five times, trying to figure out the error, but finally had to call downtown to the league office." He sees Petey streaking across the grass with the hose spewing water full blast, then times it almost perfectly. "The league office called back in an hour after checking through all their records several times. Their answer was short and to the point: 'We do not know for whom the Tells bowl.' "

A blast of water drills his chest and he falls forward, landing on his feet, then twisting and falling backward into a perfect crucifixion pose. Petey hoses him relentlessly.

God, those were the days for Willie. Days when his body was his friend; it would do anything he asked of it. Days when just *being* Willie Weaver made things happen; when Petey Shropshire and Max Craig and Eddie Single would have sold their souls to play on the same team with him, or walk into Jackie's café by his side. Days when he felt so fast and strong and confident that nothing could touch him.

— CHAPTER 2 —

On the Monday before the Crazy Horse Electric game, late in the evening, Willie and his dad take a ride. With the full moon peeking over the high eastern bluffs, Big Will backs the 700cc Honda Shadow out of the garage, coasts it down the driveway to the street, waits for Willie to slide on behind and hits the starter button. Willie hooks his thumbs in his dad's belt loops and leans back against the sissy bar, thinking how he loves the deep purr of the engine—how the power of the bike excites him. They tighten the chin straps on their helmets and Big Will eases the bike quietly down the neighborhood street to the stop sign and out the four-lane arterial toward the bluffs. At the 76 station near the edge of town, Will stops for gas and they leave the helmets—worn this far for Sandy Weaver's benefit should she happen to have been watching them leave—with the proprietor, who asks Willie if Samson Floral is going to clean up on Crazy Horse Electric on Friday.

Big Will eases the bike up to sixty as they cruise along the base of the bluffs, hidden in the long shadow from the light of the moon, then drops down a gear moving into the winding turns that will weave them the seven ribboned miles to the top. Willie leans into the turns with his dad—and with the bike—and they take each one faster than the last; shoulders closer to the highway whipping by. Moving into the tighter turns near the summit, Willie imagines they are a human wave, flowing easily from side to side in perfect synch. This would be dangerous with anybody but his dad, whom Willie sees as immortal. "Go with it," Big Will said the first time out, more than four years ago, not long after Missy's death. "Just do what the bike does."

Willie does go with it; the Shadow has taught him balance.

At the top of the bluff, on the freshly paved two-lane highway, the Shadow leaps forward as Big Will opens her up. Winding curves allow one kind of thrill, but only velocity makes it right on the straightaway. The moon rests on the horizon—as if taking a quick breather before climbing on into the night—casting the rugged high-plains scrubland in a bluish glow. The warm night wind whips through Willie's long hair, gently massaging his scalp, and at this speed he is able to close his eyes and picture the two of them from afar, cutting across the giant face of the full summer moon, tires lightly kissing the pavement; shadow dancing. His dad opens it up all the way now, and Willie leans back hard against the sissy bar, lost in the raw speed, suppressing his impulse to scream out his joy at the top of his lungs. He laughs to himself instead and shakes his head in the wind, wishing his dad could understand how close he feels when they do this.

Several quick miles into the ride along the top of the bluffs, Big Will takes a left, cuts the speed and moves the bike slowly along the narrow dirt road leading to Corbut Creek, where the two have spent hundreds of hours quietly fishing. He pulls up near their favorite hole and switches off the key, automatically cutting the light and engine. They sit, eyes adjusting to the shadowy moonlight, before Willie pulls a flashlight from the saddlebags and they move cautiously toward the bank. The moon reflects brightly off the surface of the fishing hole and Big Will motions Willie around the edge to put it at their back. They sit in the grass and Willie switches on the light, probing it deep into the water, where eventually a fish appears, then another, seeming bewildered. It would be easy to take them out; create chaos in their environment and take advantage of their confusion; but if Big Will stands for anything, it's a fair fight.

"God, look at 'em, Dad," Willie says. "I was beginning to think they'd gone South for the summer. Last two times out I been skunked."

Big Will nods, takes the light from Willie and shines it under a deep rock. A huge trout appears for an instant, then slides back into the watery darkness. "He's the one I want," he says, cutting the flashlight and leaning back on laced fingers in the grass.

"Why doesn't Mom fish with us anymore, I wonder?" Willie asks, half to himself and half to his dad; knowing if she did still fish with them and if she knew there was one that size in the creek, she'd get him, come hell or high water.

Big Will hardens, then sighs. "Guess she got tired of catching all the big ones and making you and me look like a couple of rookies."

Willie knows there's more to it than that; has to be. Mom liked fishing too much. It's one more thing somehow mysteriously connected to the day Missy died. He gathers tinder and some small sticks for a fire.

"This Crazy Horse game," Big Will says, setting a match to the tinder, "what do you think?"

"I'm excited. A *little* nervous maybe, but not bad. Mostly just excited."

"That's good. Pay real close attention to how you feel. Don't turn your attention away a minute from now till the time it's over."

"What do you mean?"

"For a month before we went to the Rose Bowl," Big Will says, "I knew it would be my game. The regular season was over and all we had to do was stay sharp until New Year's Day. I knew that was it for me. I was too small to go to the pro's and in a month I'd be out of the game for good. I dreaded it being over so much that I focused on every drill; every play called, every cut, every reception. I wanted to remember each second of my time left in football, because I didn't know if I'd ever be that good at anything again."

Willie watches his dad staring soft-eyed into the fire, running his glory days over in his head. He hears lots of Rose Bowl stories.

Big Will nods slowly. "I knew it was my game; not only that we were going to win, but that I owned it. Every day I watched it come twenty-four hours closer and I played it a different way. By game day, nothing Michigan threw at us could have surprised me."

He snaps to, glancing over to Willie, who stares back, captive.

"The point is," Big Will goes on, "that I don't just remember the game, I remember *everything* that led up to it, and in my memory the anticipation is as good as the outcome, maybe better. This won't be the end of your athletic career like the Rose Bowl was mine, but it's big enough to be worth remembering."

He touches Willie's knee. "Pay attention to everything," he says. "This could be your game."

Willie doesn't always understand everything his dad says to him, but he always listens hard because Big Will isn't a babbler; when he says something—anything—he's serious; and often the meaning comes later for Willie.

"What if it isn't?" Willie asks. "My game, I mean."

Big Will shrugs. "Then it isn't. But it won't be because you weren't ready."

They douse the fire with creek water, kick it around until the last spark is out and take the Shadow back home.

Late Wednesday afternoon, Big Will warms him up. Crouched against the six-foot wood fence in the backyard and working his twenty-year-old catcher's mitt like the mouth of a large hand puppet, he gently primes his son. "Go right after the Whitworth kid," he says. "He's the best they've got. First time up, you blow him over with fastballs. Stay in the corners; nothing too sweet."

Willie nods and moves into an exaggerated stretch, bringing his arm straight over the top almost in slow motion. The ball pops like a rifle shot in his dad's glove just like it does in Johnny's, no matter what speed the pitch. Willie and his dad have spent thousands of hours here in the backyard working on Willie's stuff; adjusting his delivery and talking about how life works. Three years ago Big Will built the regulation pitcher's mound and sunk a brand-new rubber home plate exactly sixty feet six inches away, and since then Willie has pitched inning after endless inning right here.

"Did you guys plan Missy?" Willie asks.

"What?"

"Did you plan to have her, or was she an accident?"

"You got your head in this game or what?"

"I got my head in it," Willie says. "It's just that sometimes when important things happen, I think about other important things."

It's been four years since Missy's death and Willie has discovered that sometimes, no matter how painful it is to anyone, he just has to talk about her; as if she might disappear from the family history if he didn't. They throw in silence for a while, and finally Big Will says, "What made you ask a question like that?"

"Actually, Johnny asked me that back when Mom was pregnant. Said it was strange to plan your kids twelve years apart. Thought maybe you and Mom got on a roll and forgot where you put your doodads."

"Our *doodads*?"

"Yeah. You know, whatever you use to keep from having babies."

"Ah, our doodads. I vote 'yes' on the school levy so we can have a few extras in the curriculum, like sex education, and my kid's calling contraceptive devices 'doodads.' " He fires a hard one back, but Willie catches it in the webbing and is saved the stinging hand his dad intends.

Willie leans forward, glove behind his back, squinting as if for a sign, goes into the stretch, stops and says, "Well, did you?"

"Did I what?"

"Get hot and forget your doodads. Johnny said he figured probably you guys got caught out at the drive-in or something and you let your magic whanger do your thinking for you." Willie loves those safe times when he can bait his dad.

"Johnny's going to get a soap lunch the next time I see him," Big Will says. "Now get your head into this game."

They throw awhile longer until Willie's arm feels warm and loose, then head into the house, where his dad rubs it down with heat balm. The arm is ready. Willie's ready. It's still two days to the game, but Willie's wishing it were now, forgetting for the moment his dad's advice to relish the anticipation. He'd gladly take Sal Whitworth on today. Instead he goes to the kitchen, makes up a couple quarts of lemonade and they sit in the shade and relax.

"Actually," Big Will says, "we were in a motel in Seattle, as near as I can figure. Our 'doodads' were in a drawer in Coho. If you tell Johnny Rivers that, you won't see sunrise."

Willie crosses his heart solemnly and raises his right hand. "You know your lurid secrets are always safe with me, Dad. Gimme five bucks."

Willie sways gently in the hammock and his mind runs back to Missy, like it does sometimes. It isn't so crazy anymore; not like it was right after, when he tried with all his might to force it out of his head because it was just so awful to think about. Finally his mom told him to just let it be there; let it come in when it wants to, and finally he learned to do that and then things were better. He wishes he were sure his mom could follow her own advice.

Three days after Willie's twelfth birthday, on a hot summer afternoon just before he was supposed to go to practice, his baby sister stopped breathing. Willie had gone into her room to show her off to Johnny and she was blue. He ran into the living room screaming for his mother, couldn't find her anywhere, then ran back to Missy's room and shook her. She looked less blue and he thought for a brief second she was okay, but the pasty color still wasn't right, so he ran back out, frantically searching for Eastern Montana's Mother of the Year, whose baby was dying; screaming through the house and out into the yard. His mom was standing on the sidewalk across the street talking to Mrs. Burke, and

Willie babbled Missy's name and that something was wrong, awful wrong, she was sick or maybe knocked out but that couldn't be because she was still in her crib, and his mother flew across the street and almost got hit by a car and Willie stood out by the sidewalk on their side of the street, down from the steps, under the flowering crab-apple tree that never put out any crab apples and hardly any flowers either and he heard frantic movement inside and his mother yelling. He watched her helplessly through the open door, dialing the phone, then dialing again like maybe she couldn't get the number right, and then she burst out of the house with Missy like a rag in her arms and threw her into the front seat of the car and was gone.

That was the last time Willie saw his sister. She was six months old. The doctor called it SIDS. Sudden Infant Death Syndrome.

A chink appeared that day in the Weaver family coat-of-arms; left things just a little off. They all assured each other it was no one's fault, even went to therapy for a little while over in Helena, trying to find something to do with the ugly specter of guilt that knifed into Willie's gut on its own whim, with no notice; and into his mother's gut, too. Big Will held the family together with his powerful, stoic presence, and finally time began to dull the sharp, searing edge.

But Willie could see the Weaver universe had shifted, if almost imperceptibly, like when the sound is a tiny bit off the picture. For the first time there was something Big Will couldn't take head on, something he had to turn his back on, and there seemed no way to get it back on course, really.

— CHAPTER 3 —

By the bottom of the seventh inning, the Crazy Horse Electric game belongs to Willie Weaver; it is his to win or lose. Samson Floral is ahead 1–0 on Willie's triple in the fifth, a hard drive to deep left field that scored Petey Shropshire after his second walk of the day. Crouched into his normal batting position, Petey has the strike zone of a growth-stunted Munchkin, and though he rarely hits over .200, he gets on base a lot.

Willie has had a great day on the mound so far. No batter has reached second base and only twice has he pitched to more than three hitters in an inning. His one scare came from Sal Whitworth, who tagged a pitch that got away from Willie in the bottom of the first inning, sending the ball over the left-field fence just inches outside the foul line.

Johnny's mouth, which Coach Ivy credits with being worth a run a game, is working overtime. Back in the bottom of the fifth, he called time and hustled over to the dugout to get an extra pair of socks he'd left on the bench, walked back to the plate stuffing them inside his mitt, calling loudly out to Willie, "Sorry, big boy. Didn't mean to break your concentration, but I got to have more padding. You're *hot* today, Willie boy. Hot. You hear me? Batter up! C'mon, batter. Step right up and take your medicine. We'll have you outta here in time for the early movie. Batter up! Let's get these boys outta their misery and home to their mommas. C'mon now, batter up . . ." and on and on.

The top of the ninth is quiet for Samson Floral, and

Willie goes into the last inning with a one-run lead, facing the second, third and fourth men in their batting order. Sal Whitworth bats fourth; clean-up. Between the dugout and the mound, Sal catches Willie by the arm. There's a hint of a sneer, but he says, "Throwin' good today."

Willie says, "Thanks."

"I'm catching on, though," Sal says. "Next good-lookin' pitch is outta here."

Willie won't be intimidated. "You'll get one," he says. "Count on it."

After striking out the first batter on three pitches, Willie makes his first mistake of the game. He throws a high, inside, medium fastball to back the batter off the plate some, but instead of backing down, the batter edges into it and takes the ball on his elbow, then walks to first. Willie curses himself for not throwing it harder; making the hitter pay for a freebee. That brings up Sal Whitworth for the last time and Willie knows he's flat dangerous with a runner on. Willie lets what Sal said between innings creep into his head and for the first time in the Crazy Horse Electric game he feels the slightest bit rattled.

The entire Crazy Horse team stands in the dugout screaming at him: ". . . rubber arm . . . only good for eight . . . Crazy Horse always finds a way . . . 'hon, big Sal . . ."

Willie calls time and steps off the mound. Sal smiles and steps back, too. Johnny throws off his mask and walks out to the mound at the same time Coach Ivy moves toward them from the dugout. Johnny's there first, his mouth on automatic. "Let's get rid of this guy and go home," he says. "My dad's planning a big celebration. Signing me with the Yankees if we win. C'mon, Willie, just blow him over and let's get out of here . . ."

Willie nods. "Shouldn't have hit that first batter . . ."

Coach Ivy hears him as he approaches. "Don't worry about the runner, Willie. Throw like you've been throwing and he'll die where he stands. Just concentrate on the hitter. No pick-offs. Give him all the lead he wants. Key to this game is standing right there at home plate looking at you. How's the arm? You're throwing like a champ. Feeling okay?"

Willie feels his arm. It's a little sore, maybe a hair tired. He can't tell for sure. Is this all going up in smoke in the next few pitches? Has he gone this far just to serve up the pitch that Sal Whitworth will blast into North Dakota? Willie looks past Johnny and Coach Ivy over to the stands where his dad stands in his Washington Husky football jersey, arms folded, a tight grimace on his lips. He nods at Willie: *Time to go to the well.* Willie can hear Big Will's voice over the crowd, over Johnny; because Big Will's voice is in his head. "Always go at the big guys with your best stuff, son. That's how you show 'em respect." Willie's aware this game is almost as important to his dad as it is to him; he *can't* let him down. He looks at Coach Ivy. "Arm's fine," he says.

Johnny slaps him on the butt with his mitt and says, "I'll rattle him a little," then trots back to the plate; Coach Ivy heads back to the dugout. Willie looks over to his dad again; nothing has changed.

He fools Sal with his first pitch; takes a little off it and has him reaching for Strike One. Sal nods his head, staring fiercely back at the mound, digging his cleats in deeper. The second pitch is a screamer, low and inside, which Sal takes for a ball. Then a hard fastball right down the pipe; Sal fouls it off, way, way back and out of play.

"Next one's outta here," Sal calls from the plate, and Willie smiles and nods.

Johnny's mouth is off on its own. "Hey, big Sal. Heard they're trading you soon. They're gettin' Aunt Jemima. Makes a better batter . . . Sure you wanna stay out here an' play with the big boys? . . . 'Hon, batter, your shoe's untied. Your momma's callin'; wants you home before Mr. Dream Weaver embarrasses you so bad your family has to move . . . How you ever gonna get a girlfriend after what's about to happen . . ."

Sal steps out of the box, turns around and tells Johnny to shut the hell up. Johnny shrugs. " 'Hon, Big Willie. Pitch 'er right in here. Got 'im on the run."

Sal looks to the ump, who calls batter up, and he steps back in.

Then Johnny finds Sal's weak spot. " 'Hon, Big Willie . . . got a bet with Sal here that he can't hit you. He put up his sister. I put up fifty cents. Ain't cool bettin' your sister on one swing of the bat. Not for fifty cents."

The umpire's arms shoot out to call time. "Now that's enough . . ." but before he can finish, Sal whirls around, flips Johnny's mask up, pops him three light-ning-quick open-handed blows to the side of the face and pushes him on his butt. Johnny is up like a flash and Willie charges in from the mound, but the ump steps in front of Johnny and Coach Ivy cuts Willie off.

The ump grabs Johnny's chest protector and pulls him up close. "I'd call that about even," he says. "Now you get down behind the plate and keep your mouth *shut!* One more word and you're headed for the show-ers."

Johnny says, "Yes, sir," and looks around him at Willie, who's back on the mound. Johnny smiles.

The next pitch is a statement of adolescent friendship as Willie fires a high, inside fastball right at Sal's head. Most hitters would hit the dirt, but Sal is hot and he only jerks his head back as the ball streaks by inches from his chin. The ump flips his mask up and starts to say something, but Willie puts both hands in the air and yells, "Got away from me, ump. Honest. That was an accident."

Willie looks over to his dad, who shakes his head and shoots him a disgusted look and Willie knows he shouldn't have thrown that last one. He nods at Big Will and steps up on the mound, starts into his wind-up; Sal steps out of the box. He adjusts his helmet, bangs his cleats with the bat; gives Willie time to sweat. When he stands back in, Willie steps off the mound; it works both ways. He bends down to pick up some dirt, rubs it around his hands, dusts them off and steps back up.

Willie starts into the stretch and Sal digs in. The runner on first takes a big lead off the bag, but Willie focuses completely on Sal, who's a picture of coiled determination. Willie rears back and kicks high, his arm a sling, but in the middle of his delivery he knows something is wrong; the ball slips just slightly in his fingers; he falls a hair off balance; can't pull it back. The pitch is fast and hard, but it doesn't dance, and when Sal Whitworth sees it coming, he knows it's sweet.

Sal puts everything into a powerful, level swing as Willie falls off balance, catching himself twisting toward first base, out of fielding position. He hears the crack of the bat and the ball screams straight back toward the third-base side of the mound.

Then Willie Weaver etches the Crazy Horse Electric

game in the mind of every citizen and ball player and coach—maybe every dog and cat—in Coho, Montana. From his unbalanced position, he pivots around on his left leg, *turning his back to the plate,* and *backhands* the ball out of the air. He fields a white-hot, nuclear line drive on pure instinct, robbing Sal Whitworth of a sure triple and Crazy Horse Electric of their fourth straight Eastern Montana American Legion championship. The base runner streaks toward second, his brain several steps behind events. Willie looks into his glove and smiles, waits a split second for his first baseman to catch up, then flips him the ball for the third out.

The crowd sits in stunned silence while the required synapses take place, letting them know what they've just seen really happened, then erupts. The Crazy Horse Electric game is history and Willie Weaver is a minor legend.

— CHAPTER 4 —

Willie walks into his English class on the first day of school, scans the room for a suitably obscure seat. He spots Jenny Blackburn off to one side and about halfway back, and plops his books on the desk top behind her.

"Baseball hero," she says. "How you doing?"

"Football hero," Willie corrects her. "New season, new image. Where you been? I've tried to call you for the last two weeks. You guys go on vacation?"

Jenny nods. "We went to visit my aunt in Minot. God, I think my parents take me there every year to make the first day of school look good. She watches that religious channel on TV—Trinity Network, I think they call it—the one with the blond lady who has to carry her eyelashes around in a wheelbarrow."

"Sounds like fun."

"My aunt makes *me* watch it with her. 'Jenny, honey, come in here and sit with your auntie awhile. We never talk.' So I go in and we still don't talk; we watch this lady cry and wail and praise the Lord and gush to Efrem Zimbalist Jr. and Roosevelt Grier and Tommy Lasorda. I'll bet if the real Jesus ever saw those people carrying on that way, he'd pull on his steel-toed holy boots and come down here and kick somebody's butt." She laughs. "One day I got sick of it and told my aunt those couldn't be real tears because there was no snot. When people cry for real, there's snot."

Willie laughs. "What'd she say?"

"She didn't say anything. She had a 'spell.' Lightheadedness, forearm over the forehead, calling for my father in this bullshit tremolo voice that kept my uncle on his knees for forty years before he got lucky and croaked."

Jenny goes back into what Willie imagines is a perfect imitation of her aunt. " 'Cecil, what have you done with this daughter of yours? How did you allow her to get so hateful? The devil's in this girl.' So my dad pretends to chew me out because it is *not* worth it to get on her bad side, and we end up going to church on a Thursday night—a *Thursday* night—to get the devil out of me."

"Get him out?"

Jenny smiles. "Wouldn't go."

Willie's engrossed for more reasons than are obvious, having quit worrying about preserving their friendship. He's in love. "So how is Thursday church?" he asks.

"Wretched," Jenny says. "While normal folks sit

home watching 'Cheers' and 'Hill Street Blues,' these people man the front lines against wave after wave of rock singers and poets and commie bleeding-heart liberals and 'secular humanists,' whoever *they* are." Jenny's expression changes to anger. "God, they're awful. All they really ever talk about are fear and revenge. If God was really like that, he'd be a jerk."

The loud bang of books dropped flat on the desk top across the aisle startles them. They jerk up to see Johnny Rivers sliding into his seat. "Mornin', sports fans," Johnny says, "ready to spend the next hour of your life committing the intimate details of your summer vacation to print?"

Jenny says, "We're juniors now, Rivers. They don't care what we did on our summer vacation."

"Ah, juniors," Johnny says. "A year of understudy before our time to step up and take control; bring this place to its knees. I hate it. It's limbo. I'd rather be a frosh. At least frosh have something to fight for. Their lives."

The bell rings as Mrs. Chambers walks into the room, followed closely by Petey, loaded down with books and papers. "Teacher's young slave comes bearing gifts," Willie says. Petey drops the books on her desk and heads for a seat. After a high-school career being locked in coat closets and stuffed butt-first into wastebaskets set high on book lockers, Petey stays pretty close to adults who will protect him.

Mrs. Chambers passes out twenty-nine copies of *Bless the Beasts and the Children,* saying, "I bought these out of my pocket. You each owe me a dollar and seventy-five cents. If you were to read this book and turn in a Pulitzer Prize-winning book report, and you did not pay me my dollar and seventy-five cents, the highest grade you could possibly receive would be an F." She goes on to explain that the book is about a group of misfits who seem discarded and uncared for and who have to pull together to fend for themselves and find meaning in their lives, much like the members of this class will have to do for the rest of their miserable existences, should they choose to ignore this wonderful but fleeting opportunity to acquire literacy.

"To show that somewhere deep inside me there's a feeling, caring person," she goes on, "I'm going to give you the rest of the period to read. I expect you all to finish the first three chapters by class time tomorrow. If you don't, you will find that somewhere deep inside me there's a troll."

Most students open their books and begin reading, save a few in the back two rows who are "not into readin', man." Those people fold their arms and stare at their shoes.

And Johnny. Johnny doesn't begin right away either. He stares at the cover of the book, moving his lips, closing his eyes, smiling, frowning, hitting himself gently on the forehead with the palm of his hand.

"What are you doing?" Willie whispers.

"Shhh. I've almost got it."

"Got what?"

Johnny shakes his head quickly and closes his eyes. Then he smiles with a quick, hard nod, opens the book and starts to read.

With about five minutes left in the period, he raises his hand.

"Mr. Rivers?"

Johnny stifles a smile and says, "I've been working on this idea for a book, and I was wondering if I could give just a short explanation of the plot and see if you or the rest of the class think it's got a chance."

"You've been thinking about writing a book, Mr. Rivers?"

"I know it sounds dumb," Johnny says, "and I'm embarrassed to talk about it, but I've been thinking about it all summer."

Here it comes, Willie thinks. I don't know what it is, but here it comes. Johnny Rivers has *not* spent his summer thinking about writing a book.

"It doesn't sound dumb at all, Mr. Rivers. All writers have to start somewhere. Go ahead."

"Well," Johnny starts out, "it's about this really poor family with five kids, maybe six, I haven't decided. The father works, but he only makes minimum wage and it's really tough making ends meet."

"Uh-oh," Petey says.

"What's that, Peter?"

"You better watch out," Petey says. "He's never even *read* a book, much less thought about writing one."

Mrs. Chambers looks back to Johnny, who quickly continues. "Anyway," he says, "one night in the middle of the winter, the mother goes through all the cupboards and the refrigerator, but there's just no food left. She sends one of the kids to the cellar, but all he comes back with is a partial armload of beets. The mother breaks into tears, because she just can't stand the idea of her family going hungry. Then the oldest boy remembers that there is a nest of birds up in the rafters—wrens, I think—and he crawls up and captures the mother wren and pops her noggin." Johnny makes a tight fist as if squeezing the cap off a plastic bottle.

"Ick!" Three girls in the front row feign offense.

"Sorry," Johnny says earnestly, "this is a story about

survival." He continues. "He brings the bird down and plucks it and gives it to his mom, who, though she feels bad for the wren, is grateful to have something to put on the table."

Now Petey is sure. "Stop him, Mrs. Chambers. This isn't a book. If it was a book, they'd just be birds, not 'wrens.' "

Johnny quickly breaks in before Mrs. Chambers can question him. "I don't know what he's talking about," he says. "Just lemme finish. Anyway, the bird and the vegetables are cooked and set out on the table, but the father doesn't come home. The family waits and waits, but he just doesn't appear. Fearing the bird will dry out and the dinner will spoil, the mother puts it in the refrigerator; and they wait."

"Be just a little less detailed," Mrs. Chambers says. "The bell is about to ring."

"Be a *lot* less detailed," Petey mumbles.

Johnny nods. "Okay. So, to make a long story short, the father doesn't come home till after midnight, but nobody eats because this is a close-knit religious family and they hang together. When the father washes up and is finally seated, Mom gets the bird out of the refrigerator, carves it with a small knife and distributes it equally to all the family members. Just as the kids are about to dig in, the father stops them, realizing that in their hunger they've forgotten to say grace. So they join hands around the table, bow their heads and the father speaks." Johnny looks up at Mrs. Chambers and smiles. "You know what he says?"

Petey says, "Oh, God. Somebody lock me in the coat closet."

"This doesn't sound like a story plot at all," Mrs. Chambers says. "Mr. Rivers, what exactly is this about?"

"You know what he says?" Johnny asks, getting more excited by the second. "He says, 'Dear Lord, bless the beets and the chilled wren.'" He squeals and pounds his head against his desk. "Get it? Bless the beets and the chilled wren. *Bless the Beasts and the Children.* Get it? God, that's *great!* I must be precocious. I made that up myself. Just now."

The rest of the class is groaning. "On our baseball team we get him for this," Petey says. "We pants him or hose him down or something."

"I don't doubt it a bit," Mrs. Chambers says, smiling. "If this weren't a free country, Mr. Rivers would be in an internment camp in a very cold place for a very long time."

"Bless the beets and the chilled wren," Johnny says, and bangs his forehead on the desk again. "That's *great.*"

The bell rings. "That's all for today, class. Everyone but Mr. Rivers is excused."

Dinner was late tonight because football practice ran longer than usual. Willie and Jenny have taken the new highway to the top of the bluffs on their ten-speeds and now pedal single file along the ridge top, looking down over Coho in the late summer sunset. Willie's stomach is jittery; he plans to make the change in their relationship if he can, but doesn't have a *clue* how to pull it off. Girls have always liked him, but Jenny's special.

They turn onto the Corbut Creek road, and Willie leads her to his fishing hole.

"You think Johnny has some kind of brain disease?" Jenny asks, as she leans her bike against a large tree and plops down in the grass beside Willie.

"No question about it, I think. I just hope it's terminal.

And quick. Until today, there was a finite number of those things. Now that he's found out he can make them up, no one is safe."

Jenny peers into the dark water. "This is your fishing hole, huh? You pull a lot of big ones out of here?"

"Not lately, but it's been pretty good over the last few years. Dad and I came up the other night and checked it out with a flashlight. There's still lots of fish, they're just getting smart. They're lucky my mom retired. She was the best fisherman I ever saw. She could pull rainbow trout out of a sump."

"Why'd she quit?"

Willie wants to talk about *them*—Jenny and him—not about his mother the retired angler; but he senses bad timing. "I don't know," he says. "It's funny, I never thought about it before the other night, but I think it had something to do with my baby sister dying. I don't think she's been fishing since that day."

Jenny is quiet. She remembers how Willie took himself away for several months after his sister died from SIDS; how she tried everything she knew to get through to him, but he was just gone. Absent from the world. She wants to ask about that, but doesn't. She's sixteen and the mystery of death is magnetic to her, and Missy's death is the only one, so far, that's been close to her in any way. Willie knows more of the mystery, but Jenny has a strong sense of privacy.

They stare into the dark fishing hole and finally Willie says, "When somebody's still blue, you can save them."

"What?"

"Missy was blue when I saw her first. Remember in Lifesaving class this summer? They said when some-body's still blue, it means they haven't been not breathing for very long. If I'd known how to do CPR, I could have saved Missy. She was blue. Missy could still be alive and my mother could still be fishing."

Jenny moves over close and lays a hand on Willie's knee. "You were only twelve . . ."

Willie nods. "I know. I just wish they told you things when you need them. It seems like they always tell you things when it's too late."

From the side, Jenny puts her arms around his shoulders and nuzzles into his neck. "You been thinking about that all this time?"

"Not all the time. I've only known that a few months; and I don't really think about it when I'm busy. But sometimes when my mom doesn't know I'm watching, she looks so *sad* I can hardly stand it. That's when I think about it."

Jenny holds him tighter. All the tense, unspoken messages dissipate like fog in the hot sun, and Willie knows he doesn't have to tell Jenny how he feels. He's opened a door, and she's waltzed right in. "You want to go with me?" she says.

"Huh?"

"Go with me. You know, dances, holding hands, stuff like that."

Willie doesn't hesitate. "Yeah, I do. I do wanna go with you."

She kisses him on the cheek. "Okay," she says, "but you gotta give me something."

"Like what?"

"I don't know. A VCR. A car maybe."

Willie pushes her away to get a better look. "How about my American Legion Championship ring?"

"That would do for now. Till you can save up some money." She kisses him again, this time lightly on the mouth. "Let's get going. I've got to be home before dark."

Heading into the long, steep slope back to town, Jenny pedaling directly behind him, Willie hears the metallic click of her derailleur gears shifting into high. "Oh, Christ," he says, closing his eyes momentarily and reaching to the crossbar for his own gears.

Jenny shoots by him as if out of a giant sling, Chinese braid whipping in the wind, yelling, "See you later, baseball hero!"

He shifts into high, pouring it on, but Jenny's pulling away. He knows he'll catch her, but Jenny Blackburn was born on that bike.

Halfway down the grade, Jenny is no longer widening the gap, and as they near the three-quarter mark, Willie starts to gain. His thighs burn like molten steel and his lungs and stomach ache; but he's gaining. Three hundred yards from the bottom, his front tire is even with Jenny's rear tire. She's leaning forward as far as gravity will allow and pedaling like a runaway locomotive, but slowly Willie's tire pulls even with her crossbar. His legs pump as fast as he can make them; he leans farther into it, his wheel now even with the back of her front tire.

Then, fifty yards from the bottom of the hill, Jenny suddenly sits back and throws up her arms in triumph. "Finish!" she yells. "She does it again, folks. Jenny Blackburn does it again! Her opponent today, a virtual unknown, gave her a tremendous push, but Jenny was equal to the challenge. Seldom in cycling history . . ."

"Okay, okay," Willie puffs, coasting beside her as they shoot out onto the flat. "You win. You always win. You always will win, as long as you race these courses with the flexible finish line."

"So you want to tamper with the rules?" she asks,

shaking her head in disgust. "Typical rookie behavior on this circuit."

They pedal back into town as dusk turns to a dark brownish gray, and Jenny turns off at her street, yelling back over her shoulder, "Looks like you worked up a pit! Make sure you get a shower. I like my boyfriend clean."

— CHAPTER 5 —

Willie tightens down the boat-trailer hitch and wraps the safety chain twice around the bumper of the Bronco, then tests it, jerking up hard on the tongue of the trailer. Good and tight. He waves to his dad, who eases the boat down the driveway and into the street, then backs up until the Bronco stands in front of the walk running to the house. Sandy hurries out the door with a giant picnic basket and several blankets, followed by Johnny Rivers carrying wetsuits and water skis, which he deposits in the boat, then hops into the backseat with Willie.

"What time's Jenny expecting us to pick her up?" Big Will asks, pulling out onto the street.

"Whenever," Willie says. "She gets up around six to run or ride her bike, so she'll be ready."

"Coulda swore I saw an American Legion Championship ring on her finger the other day," Johnny said. "Wonder where she got that. Think she's going steady with Petey?"

Willie says, "Keep it up, buddy."

"That wasn't yours, was it?" Johnny stays with it as if he didn't hear. "Two jocks in budding romance? That's dangerous. Somebody could get beaned . . ."

Willie threatens a budding nosebleed, and Johnny laughs. "I been slapped around by Sal Whitworth, remember? Toughest guy in three states. Popped me three times before I could get to the ground. You think I care about a little nosebleed?"

"Mouth like you've got," Big Will says, "you can probably expect a lot more Sal Whitworths in your life before you're old enough to vote."

"Everybody says that," Johnny says. "Nobody appreciates rapier-like wit anymore."

Willie's mom says, "Sometimes you just don't know when to quit, Johnny. Like in the Crazy Horse game when you started in on that Whitworth boy's sister."

"Yeah," Johnny says. "Cut that kinda close, didn't I? Guess that's what makes me so cute. Always out there walking the edge. Besides, I know when to quit. If he'd have knocked me cold, I'd have quit."

Jenny's waiting on her porch as the Bronco pulls up, and she jumps up and runs down the walk, jerks open the back door and hops in. She pecks Willie on the cheek, catching Johnny's look as she does; squints menacingly, and shakes her fist at him.

"See?" Johnny says. "I know when to quit."

Big Will stays on the freeway as long as he can, then turns onto the two-lane highway leading to Salmon Lake. It's the last weekend they'll be able to get to the lake, the last weekend of water sports until next summer. Already nights are occasionally down to freezing and the water will be cold, which is the reason for the wetsuits, but the Weavers stretch summer out as long as they can. Winter in eastern Montana can be long and cruel.

Big Will turns the conversation to football. Coho High School won its fourth game out of five yesterday and Willie's name is starting to hit the papers. It's been mentioned more than once whose son he is.

Jenny teases him about an alley-oop pass he threw into the end zone yesterday for an interception. The defender ran it back clear to midfield before Willie could bring him down.

"Coach said I should train to be a basketball ref," Willie laughs. "Throw jump balls." He shakes his head. "That was supposed to be for Mike Johnson. I figured if I could get it into the end zone, he could just jump up and catch it. Jeez, he's six four."

"Yeah," Big Will says, "but the ball must have been in the air seven seconds. You got more hang time than most punters." Then, more seriously, "That was pretty funny because you guys won it anyway, but those kinds of mistakes can kill you. Never do less than your best just because you're playing an inferior team."

"It *slipped*," Willie says defensively. "I just lost my grip."

Johnny laughs. "God, it was high enough you could have run down and caught it yourself."

"Would have saved the interception," Jenny says.

"Yeah, well, it was a bad call."

"The bad call," Sandy says, "was the one you screamed out when the ball slipped out of your hand. Where do you hear language like that?"

Willie points. "Jenny."

"It should have been short and over the middle to me," Johnny says.

Willie says, "Absolutely."

"Wouldn't have had to embarrass your mother the nun with scatological epithets."

"Absolutely," Sandy says.

Big Will stares at the road. "Never do less than your best."

The landing at Salmon Lake is empty. A power boat races by about fifty yards out as they back the trailer into the water, and there's one ski boat in sight, but other than that, the Weavers are the only party in town. Big Will and Jenny lower the boat from the trailer to the water while Johnny and Willie and Sandy unload the car and set up in a nearby picnic area.

"Gonna fish today?" Willie asks his mom as they move the barbecue grill in under the trees and set it on its stand.

"I might," she says, "when you're all finished skiing. Your dad and I talked about maybe cutting you three loose on the beach for a bit while we troll."

Willie hopes that happens.

Johnny's voice jars him from his thoughts. "I remember we came up to this lake when I was a little kid," he says. "My brother and I thought there was sunken treasure and we brought our snorkels and goggles and fins and spent the whole day just swimming around with our faces in the water looking for something shiny."

Sandy is sucked in. "Find any?" she asks jokingly.

Johnny smiles. "Matter of fact, we did. After we'd swam around almost all day and finally given up, we took off our gear and were wading in and I bashed into something hard with my lower leg."

"And it was sunken treasure."

"It was. Really. Just goes to show, sometimes booty is only shin deep."

Big Will fires the ski-rope handle at him, and Johnny ducks, then smiles, pounding his chest like Tarzan.

"He can get you anytime," Jenny tells Sandy. "Never ask him anything about anything."

"C'mon, you guys," Johnny says, "I'm just a kid who's maturing process is permanently arrested, and, besides, I'm not responsible. You think I tell those things because I want to? You oughta hear what it's like inside my head. It's *noisy*. So indulge me, I'm a sick boy. Give ol' Johnny Rivers a little round of applause when you hear one of those. He's just out here doin' his best."

Big Will hops into the boat to crank up the engine, eases it away from the dock and takes a short warm-up spin while the kids pull on the wetsuit tops. Willie stands on the edge of the dock smiling and thinking how he loves speed as his dad opens the engine full-bore.

"Don't get too taken by fast things." His mom's voice comes from behind, and he turns around to see her watching him; Jenny a few steps back. "They can hurt you. One of these days you and your dad may have to pay for all your recklessness."

Willie smiles. "We're careful," he says. "We just like to go fast."

Sandy looks into him. "You're careful?" she says, raising her eyebrows. "You think I don't know where you leave your helmets when you take the bike up on the bluffs?" She shakes her head. "You guys think you're so so smart. Telling Mr. Cantrall at the 76 station anything is like putting it in the newspaper."

Willie sees a flash of the sadness he sometimes sees in his mother's eyes. Missy's sadness. "I've lost all I can afford to lose," she says, almost matter-of-factly, and

Willie has no words. He makes a mental note to tell his dad they need to leave their helmets somewhere else.

Big Will pulls the boat up next to the dock and throws out the ski rope. "Need a skier and a spotter," he yells.

Johnny already has the ski on and Willie looks around for a ski vest, which is nowhere to be found. From the Bronco he yells that they only have the extra-large; the others must be home on the porch. Johnny nearly swims in the extra-large, but he cinches it as best he can and grabs the rope handles.

"Why don't you ride in the boat and spot, Mom?" Willie says. "Jenny and I'll set up the food."

Sandy doesn't argue, just smiles and steps over the side into the boat, pinching Big Will as she gets in. "Hey, big boy," she says. "Let's dump this bugger somewhere out in the deep water and go for a nice boat ride."

"Can't be done," Johnny says smugly, standing on the dock, measuring the slack in the rope. "I'm the Muhammad Ali of fresh-water sports."

Big Will says, "We'll see," as he shoves the boat into gear and idles forward.

When the slack is almost up, Johnny screams, "Hit it, Ski Cat!" and Big Will shoves the throttle forward full speed. Johnny steps off the dock onto the water, barely wetting his feet. Within seconds he is cutting across the wake, shooting a high rooster tail. Jenny and Willie hear him challenging Big Will to "Dump me! Dump me!" as they walk back toward the picnic table, Willie with his arm draped easily across her shoulders.

When the table is nearly set, Willie heads up the trail to the public outhouses, lost in the crunching of the pine needles beneath his feet on the trail and the crispness of the day; the brilliant colors of fall. He stops to take a leak, then walks farther from the water, thinking about his mother: how she hides her pain; how sort of disrespectful he and his dad have been, not paying better attention; and for some reason memories of Missy rush in, filling his chest, almost choking him. Startled by their power, he turns around.

Back with Jenny, the feeling fades.

Out on the water, Johnny flips the rope in the air, glides toward the dock, turns and sits. His wake catches up and washes over his legs as Willie and Jenny trot toward him.

"It's *great!*" he says, working his way out of the too-large jacket and kicking the ski loose. "Colder'n a welldigger's butt in the Klondike, but great."

Willie takes a turn, then Jenny, then Big Will. Sandy isn't a skier, so she takes the rope and spotter duties; drives the boat when Big Will skis. They eat, then the kids stay on shore to catch the last of the autumn sun while Will and Sandy take a slow tour of the lake, throw out a fish line.

Willie's on his stomach at the end of the dock, head and neck over the edge, peering into the deep green water at a school of minnows jerking this way and that, as if to the snap of a minnow-trainer's whip. Johnny gathers a dozen or so flat rocks, skips them out onto the lake. The water is rougher as the breeze picks up, making it harder to skip the rocks, but Johnny gets three or four out of even his worst throws, uttering a loud "Ha!" when he gets more. Jenny moves over to Willie, sits cross-legged beside him and begins to run her fingernails gently across his back.

Willie groans under the gentle pressure of her touch, a trick he learned watching Big Will get the most out of a back rub from Sandy. His mom can't quit when his dad obviously enjoys it so much. Jenny watches Big Will and Sandy putter slowly parallel to the shore. Then, softly, "Your mom and dad really love each other, don't they?"

Willie nods. "I think so."

"I think they have a marriage like I want. Only one I've ever seen."

"What about *your* folks?"

"My folks just look good in public. Sometimes I don't think they even really like each other. I mean, when one of your parents does something on their own, it seems right. It's like they're sort of proud of each other for having their own lives. I don't think either one of my folks even knows what the other one likes."

"That's crappy," Willie says.

"Crappy for them. They're nice to me, though, so I guess I shouldn't complain. But sometimes it seems like it wouldn't even matter if they split up. I mean, sometimes I sort of wish they'd have boyfriends and girlfriends or something; something that would make their lives exciting. God, I hope my life is never like that."

Johnny has moved into earshot and for the first time today he's serious. "That doesn't always work out so great either," he says. "Two years ago my mom found out my dad was screwing around with some woman down at his office. About three minutes into *that* conversation I was ready for something less exciting."

"Your dad was screwing around?" Jenny asks. "God, what'd you do?"

"Took my little brother and headed for high ground."

Jenny leans back on her hands and nods. "Yeah," she says. "Maybe it's as bad one way as another."

They look up to the sound of the boat idling their way about twenty feet from the dock. The sun is low, just above the mountains. "One last run?" Big Will yells. "Summer's almost over."

"I'll go one more," Willie says, pulling the wetsuit top on. Sandy asks Jenny to ride in the boat as spotter while she and Johnny load the Bronco. Willie straps the life jacket on over the wetsuit, trying in vain to find a way to take up the slack of its size. "God," he says, "I hate this thing. Why don't I go without it, Dad? The wetsuit will keep me up."

Big Will shakes his head. "No jacket, no go. You know the rule."

Willie straps it on as his dad idles slowly straight out from the dock. Jenny pitches him the rope. He stands with his foot in the ski until the slack is up, then yells, "Hit it!" and the boat shoots forward, pulling him effortlessly onto the water. The wind is higher, the lake rougher, and Willie works hard to keep his rudder in the water as he cuts sharp curves and flies across the wake. Twice he's almost upended, but manages to right himself. He waves to get Jenny's attention and draws a big circle in the air with his finger, a message Jenny relays to his dad, and Big Will takes the boat in a long, wide curve. Willie crouches down, pointing the ski directly away from the boat to crack the whip, and as the boat circles tighter, he flies faster in its arc. It takes all his strength to hold on against the centrifugal force, but he grips the handle tighter, crouches even lower, pulling into a wider, faster orbit. The ski slaps loudly on the rough water as the waves shoot under him, and he leans back to hold the rudder down. The speed and the wind in his face and the sheer power of it all send adrenaline through him like a river, and his yell is drowned out by the noise of the engine and the wind and the water juggling him across its surface.

His shoulders ache and his back leg begins to numb, so he stands to cut back in toward the boat, but his weight shifts forward and a wave splashes over the tip of the ski, forcing it down and pitching Willie forward. The tip bounces back up in time to catch him in the middle of the forehead and the last thing he sees is blood from a gash ripped to the bone. The life jacket slips up, trapping his arms and head, and Willie slips into darkness.

Jenny knows instantly Willie's hurt and screams to Big Will, who immediately cuts a tight circle back, whipping the boat around to get close. He sees Willie's head below water and dives in as Jenny braces herself on the side, ready to pin Willie's hands so Big Will can crawl back into the boat to pull him up, like she learned in their Lifesaving class, but Big Will keeps pushing him up from in the water, and the boat floats lazily away. Jenny tries to help, yells instructions, but Big Will seems stricken, near panic. "Get his hands where I can reach!" Jenny screams, but he ignores her, pulling Willie back toward him, working to free him from the tangled jacket.

"He's not breathing!" Big Will screams. "He's not breathing! Oh, God, no! Not again!"

"Get him over here!" Jenny screams again, to Big Will's deaf ears. She jumps into the icy water, treading momentarily as she gasps for breath, then swims toward them. Big Will looks disoriented, completely confused. His efforts to free Willie from the jacket are tangling him worse; Willie's head is in and out of the water like a bobber on a fish line, and the blood from his forehead makes the scene look like something from *Jaws*. Jenny maneuvers herself behind Willie, grabs hold of the back of his life jacket, places her foot in the middle of Big Will's chest and kicks as hard as she can, prying the two of them apart. In a quick move she pulls the vest partway open, unravels the strap caught on the wetsuit and Willie's head comes free. Immediately she begins mouth-to-mouth resuscitation, all the while kicking away from Big Will, who is lunging toward them. She screams, "Stop it! Stop it!" between breaths. "Goddam it, *please* stop it!" and finally Big Will hears her; sees her forearm braced under Willie's neck; imagines her breathing life back in.

He stops as if slapped into consciousness. "Okay, okay. I'm okay. Is he breathing? Tell me if he's breathing."

Jenny looks up between breaths. "Get the boat," she says and puts her mouth back over Willie's.

Still stunned, Big Will swims to the boat, pulls himself in and cranks the engine. Above the roar, he hears Jenny scream, "He's breathing! He's breathing! It works! Oh, God, it works! He's alive!"

The boat is left in the water; the Bronco speeding for Lambert, the nearest town with a hospital. A shivering Jenny sits in the backseat with Willie's head on her lap, running her fingers through his wet hair. Willie's mother is in shock beside them, but she moves the blanket up around Willie's shoulders, the way she tucked him in when he was three. Johnny can't stop shaking in the front seat, his eyes glued to the road, as the sun drops like a rock, leaving the eastern Montana landscape shrouded in a dank grayish brown.

Willie hasn't regained consciousness.

— CHAPTER 6 —

Willie pulls on two pairs of sweats in the early-morning darkness of his room, then feels his way to the closet and down under the pile of dirty clothes for his Nikes. The temperature outside is well below zero, and he digs out extra socks, his gloves and a pullover ski mask. The digital clock over his bed says five-thirty. He feels his way downstairs and through the kitchen, already sweating under the load of clothing, then out the back door to the alley. He bends down to stretch out his legs, leaning curiously to his right. Three months out of balance. The first three months of the rest of his life. "Use it," Dr. Swanson had said when Willie asked him how he could get his body to work right again. "I have no idea how much you can get back because we're not sure what the damage is, or where it is. These things are unpredictable. The only way you'll ever know is to work it and work it and work it. The human brain has an amazing ability to compensate. When one part shuts down, often another part covers for it. But you have to work it constantly to let that other part know what it's compensating *for.*"

So finally Willie is running. Two months it took him to muster the courage to leave the house. He faked terrible headaches to stay home from school so the other kids wouldn't see him this way, but one day Big Will came into his room and said that, headaches or no headaches, Willie was by God going to get back with it. Enough was enough.

He went to school late that first day; walked through

the doors after the bell so he could negotiate the hall and the lockers and the stairs in relative obscurity; forgo explanations.

They clapped when he pushed the door open with his cane and limped to his desk in first-period English. Johnny and Petey ran up and slapped him on the back as if he'd just pitched the final out in the Crazy Horse Electric game; and Jenny put her hand on his arm and cried. She was the only one who had actually heard how he talked now; or how he didn't talk. She had watched him work so hard for his words, felt the pain of wanting to help, to talk for him in those long silences when he struggled to get what was in his head out through his mouth; watched the beads of sweat break on his forehead as his stomach tightened, his throat constricted, pushing, forcing the words out. But that day, his first back, Willie just said "Hi" to everyone and sat at his desk like it was a cocoon. His classmates were *so* careful; Willie felt pitied.

This morning Willie decides to go for a mile and a half. His gait is uneven; right side jogging, left side following—dragging. There is no rhythm, no way to breathe evenly. He has a purpose in running this early in the day: It's dark; no one will see. As he gets in better shape, able to run farther, and as the days get longer, he'll run earlier. He envisions the neighbors looking out their windows at the Weaver cripple stumbling by; shaking their heads, telling each other what a shame, he had so much potential. No way. Willie will run in the dark.

The so-called "run" takes him nearly half an hour. Nothing about it feels athletic, nothing pleasing. Used to be Willie ran and his whole being fell into a cadence;

a rhythm in which he dreamed his dreams of glory for miles. Now he only wants to get it over with, get into the safety of his bathroom; turn out all the lights and let the hot water wash over him. He lives his days from sanctuary to sanctuary: his dark shower, the back room in the school library, even the toilet stalls in the rest room. Sometimes between classes he goes there to sit, pretending to be constipated so he can just have that time. Within a week of the day his dad shoved him back into the world, Willie had scouted out all the caves.

"I was wondering if you'd be interested in taking over the team-manager position for girls' basketball." Mr. Walker has called Willie into his office during study hall. "Allen Silver has to quit because his dad wants him to work after school. Coach and I thought you might like to get around sports again."

Willie pauses before speaking. He's learning he has to hear himself inside his head first; sometimes even see the words. "I don't . . . know. I'll . . . have to . . . think . . . about it." It's embarrassing, especially around adults, to be so *slow.* He *thinks* fast enough . . .

"Well, Willie, it's certainly up to you, but consider you've been around athletics all your life. It might be just what you need."

Up to now, Willie thinks, athletics was a friend. He doesn't try to say it; just nods his head. "Thanks," he says, and limps back through the outer office, banging his leg against the paper cutter on the counter; feeling his blood flush to his face as Mr. Walker's secretary smiles. *God, if people would just quit* smiling *at me all the time,* he thinks. *What the hell do they think I want to see anyone smiling for?* He pictures himself wiping the smile off the secretary's face with his fist, and gives a

little satisfied snort. In these three months, anger has
built to rage inside him and there's no release.

Johnny catches up to him in the hall, slows his pace to
match Willie's. "Up for a party?" he says.

Willie looks at him as if Johnny were cat poop in the
middle of his bedspread.

"C'mon," Johnny says. "What're you gonna do, never
go to another party?"

Willie's eyes get big and he nods vigorously. "That's
. . . right," he says, and thinks: *You turd. That's exactly
right. I'm never going to another party. What the hell is
the matter with you?* But he only nods faster.

"Bullcrap," Johnny says. "I'm having a party at my
place on Friday night. Parents will be in Helena. All
people you know; ball players and stuff. Jenny's going to
pick you up."

Willie breathes a big sigh and sets his jaw.

Tears well in Johnny's eyes. "Weaver, you're *still* the
guy that put it to Sal Whitworth. Every guy on the team
knows why he has a championship ring. It's not your
fault you got hurt." He wipes his eyes furiously. "I'm
your friend, man. I wanna stay your friend, but I don't
know what to *do*. Really. Just tell me what to do. I been
running around being careful and trying to make it so
you don't have to talk and backing off just like everyone
else. But if I were you and everybody treated me like
that, I'd hate it, and I'm supposed to be your friend and
I don't want to be like that. So just tell me what to do,
God damn it."

Willie looks at Johnny and leans against the wall,
shaking his head; takes a deep breath and lets it out. His
anger drains out through his feet, and he just feels sorry.
"I . . . don't . . . know," he says carefully. "I . . .
want you . . . friend. I . . . don't know." He glances

at the hall clock. The bell will ring in less than a minute and pack the halls with kids changing classes. He wants to get away.

"Will you come to the party?" Johnny asks.

Willie flashes on how awful he's been to his friends since the accident. He closes his eyes and nods. "Yeah."

His next class is speech therapy, which isn't actually in a classroom, but in one of the counselors' offices. The school district provides a traveling speech therapist and Willie was plugged into an hour a week of her time the day he got back. He likes her and he's relieved to have one period where there are no other kids, though he doesn't feel it's really doing any good. He can't talk all that much better right now than he could the day he came out of the coma. So far, she's only worked on trying to relax him.

"Did you work on those exercises I gave you last time?" she asks, noticing he hasn't brought any books or papers.

He starts to nod, but then shakes his head.

"Answer me in words, Willie."

Willie says, "No."

"Why not?"

"I . . . just . . . didn't . . . get around . . . to it."

"You didn't get around to it. You have a full social schedule to keep or something? Have to go to the horse races? What do you mean you didn't get around to it?"

Willie looks off to the side, at the floor, and sighs. "I . . . just didn't . . . do . . . it."

Ms. Jackson puts her hand on his hand; the bad one. "Willie, don't you *want* to get better? Do you want to feel like this forever? Because you're going to if you don't do something about your speech."

He looks at the floor again and shakes his head. "I don't . . . care."

Ms. Jackson gets up and quickly puts her materials into her briefcase. "Well then," she says softly, "you're wasting your time and mine, too. I have a whole bunch of kids on my roster who do care, and they're the ones I can do something about. You let your counselor know if you change your mind." She walks out, closing the door quietly behind her.

Willie stands up to stop her, tell her he's sorry, that he'll try harder, but he catches his good leg on the corner of the table and a searing pain shoots through his thigh. He kicks the table and falls, lies there a moment and lets the rage come up through his throat; a guttural roar that is the only thing he has to release his pain. The sounds of his agony die in the soundproofed walls and cushion-tiled ceiling. No one comes to his rescue. He pulls himself up and into his chair, where he sits until the period is over.

Friday, Jenny pulls her father's car up in front of the Weaver house, hits the horn and hops out to go to the door. Sandy greets her there. "He's not quite ready yet, Jenny. Come on in." Jenny comes in and sits on the couch, across from the chair where Big Will is alternately reading the evening paper and watching "People's Court" on television. She can't understand why Mr. Weaver seems so distant since the day of the accident.

"Do you think that's real?" she asks, looking at the fat woman on the screen whose million-dollar AKA Shih Tzu has been violated by the plaintiff's junkyard mongrel, thereby adding sludge to its royal gene pool until the end of time. A classic case of breeding above one's station; a Class A felony.

"What's that?"

" 'People's Court.' Do you think it's real?"

Big Will gives a half-smile. "I like to hope not. I'm not really watching it, I just didn't turn the set off after the news."

"I hope this party helps," Sandy says, sitting at the dining-room table with a cup of coffee. Big Will goes back to the paper; Jenny feels the tension she's felt every time over here since the accident—maybe not *tension* really, but at least pressure. Like a headache that doesn't quite work its way into your consciousness; always just below the surface, but definitely there if you stop to notice. Life in the Weaver house has a sense of unraveling; frayed edges that could go any time. Someone should pay attention.

"Hi," Willie says from the top of the stairs, then moves slowly down. "You . . . ready?"

Jenny rises and nods. "Sure am," she says, and moves over to meet him, kissing him on the cheek. "You look real nice."

Willie nods. "Too bad . . . it . . . isn't . . . a costume . . . party."

She punches him lightly. "Don't start," she says. "You do look real nice."

Johnny answers the door and within seconds all Willie's old buddies are gathered around him, wanting him to feel comfortable, trying too hard, and Willie feels the added burden of trying to make *them* comfortable with *his* condition. Jenny's radar picks it up and she pushes him through the kitchen into the living room, where MTV blasts from the twenty-five-inch stereo console

TV. A few people dance, but most stand around drinking soda and talking. Johnny pops Willie a Coke and moves the chips and dip within his reach. In a short while Willie is surprised to find that it's not so bad; that things get close to normal once the initial discomfort has passed, and he feels himself enjoying watching, though he can't participate really, not like he used to. He realizes how he's isolated himself over the past months, and for a quick second vows to contact Ms. Jackson first thing on Monday and promise he'll work. That vow will come and go a thousand times in the next weeks.

At ten-thirty Petey shows, complaining vehemently about having to attend his sister's piano recital before his parents would turn him loose. "That's what's wrong with music people," he says. "It isn't that they want you to practice all the time and never go out and have any fun, it's that they want your whole family to suffer right along with you. I wouldn't mind if my sister ate her meals at the piano; in fact, I'd *rather* she ate her meals at the piano; I just don't think I should have to pay because she wants to be the first female Van Clayberg or whatever his name is. I don't make her play baseball. Hey, Willie! You came. That's neat. How you doin'?"

Willie smiles and nods. "Okay."

Petey gets a Coke from the kitchen and comes to sit beside Willie and Jenny on the couch. He looks at Jenny, then right into Willie's eyes, and a huge sadness crosses his face. He says, "Are you going to get better, Willie?" Petey is nothing if not direct.

There's a silence as Willie stares into his lap. He doesn't know the answer. He doesn't know if he'll get better. Finally, without looking up, he says, "Yeah. I . . . have to. I . . . can't . . . get worse."

Willie finds a comfort zone as the evening wears on. His friends relive the Crazy Horse Electric game with him and he mostly just listens.

"When Whitworth started hammering on my head after I trashed his sister," Johnny says, "all I thought was 'I hope they won't let a convicted murderer have his turn at bat.'" They laugh and Willie remembers his decision to throw the next pitch at Sal's head; a decision which luckily had no consequence, but still one he regrets.

The dining-room rug is rolled back and more people begin dancing. Johnny gets up to dance with his date and the others break up either to get more refreshments or to dance, leaving Jenny and Willie alone. Jenny's fingernails trace lightly over the back of Willie's neck, and goosebumps pop up all over his body; he leans into her touch.

"Dance?" A hand is in front of them. Willie looks up to see Charles Boots, an offensive lineman on the varsity.

Jenny starts to shake her head, but Willie looks at her and nods. "If . . . you don't . . . you . . . might . . . never . . . get to." He pauses and breathes out, "It's . . . okay."

Jenny stands up and glides out onto the floor without taking Charles' hand. Charles holds back, checking it out with Willie. "I just thought she might want to . . ."

Willie nods and raises his hand. "It's . . . okay. Thanks."

All Willie's fears loom over him as he watches Jenny move. She dances like she does everything else physical —with barely controlled abandon. He's not worried about Charles Boots. He just knows if she stays with Willie she won't get to do much. Pretty soon she'll drift away. Just as soon as she stops feeling sorry for him. A sweeping, sinking feeling washes over him. If they had remained just friends, it wouldn't matter. Jenny could be nice to him and do some things with him, whatever he could do, and still not have to give up everything for him.

There's a loud knock, and before anyone can answer it, the kitchen door swings open, revealing Martin Cross and a few of his friends. Martin has a case of beer, and one of his buddies cradles a paper sack under one arm, obviously full of hard liquor. "Johnny!" Martin yells. "You're havin' a party. You didn't invite me. I'm hurt."

Johnny stops dancing and walks toward the kitchen. "How you guys doin'?" he asks. "Actually, I didn't think you'd want to come. Almost everyone here is in training. No goodies." Johnny is sort of the link between the jocks and the stoneys at Coho. He likes to party in the off season and he has a lot of friends that most of the athletes steer clear of.

"Heard your parents are out of town," Martin says. "Thought it might be all right if we came over. We won't corrupt anyone, honest. Promise. No jocks get no booze."

If there's a word missing from Johnny Rivers' vocabulary, it's "no." He thinks a minute, knows it's a mistake, but hopes not a very big one. "Okay," he says finally, "but I'm tellin' you, Cross—things get screwed up, I get my butt in a sling, and you're a dead man."

Marty crosses his heart. "Hey, man, no sweat." He and his buddies break out some beers, stash the rest in the refrigerator and take over a corner of the kitchen, away from the rest of the party.

Jenny plops down beside Willie at the dying strains of a hot Bob Seger rock-and-roll tune, beads of sweat standing out on her forehead, and kisses him, stroking his fingers. He smiles, but in his head he sees her going away; sees them on the dance floor together, Jenny moving with the grace of the natural athlete she is, Willie bucking and lurching, aided by his cane; a complete ass.

Johnny sits down and Jenny corners him. "What are Cross and his buddies doing here?"

"They're okay," Johnny says defensively. "They're gonna stay out of the way. They're just looking for a place to hang out for a while."

Jenny shakes her head. "They've got booze, Johnny. You know what would happen if this party got busted right now. Every kid here would be in deep, muddy water. You know the rules, man."

Johnny's eyes roll. "Geez, Jen. We're not gonna get busted. Why would anybody bust us? Cops don't even know my parents are gone. Neither does anyone at school. Who's gonna look for trouble here? We're not the bad guys. They're not hurting anything."

"Marty Cross is trouble," Jenny says. "If something happens, I'm going to be *really* pissed at you, Johnny."

"Well, I don't want you pissed at me, so I'll make sure nothing happens." As if to be sure, Johnny sticks his head into the kitchen to check on Marty and his friends.

"Is it really okay if I dance once in a while?" Jenny asks. "I'll stop if you want. It's really no big deal . . ."

Willie raises his hand. "It's . . . okay . . . Best . . . really."

She runs her fingernails lightly over the back of his neck again and he feels tears welling up in his eyes. He looks away. "Bathroom," he says. With the aid of the arm of the couch, he stands and limps off through the kitchen to the bathroom.

On his return through the kitchen, he stands for a second at the door. Jenny is dancing with Johnny and he turns back toward the sink for a glass of water.

"Hey, Willie Weaver," Marty says from the table.

Willie looks at him and nods.

"Hey, man, really sorry about what happened to you. Tough break."

At first Willie thinks Marty is being sarcastic; chiding him. Marty has never been a friend of the jocks. But when he looks into his eyes, he sees Marty's sincere.

Marty catches his look. "Really, man. Hate to see anybody lose his best stuff. You were really somethin', man. My big brother saw that championship baseball game. Still talks about your catch. Hate to see a guy lose his best stuff. Sorry, man."

Willie nods and starts to walk away, but feels a strange draw to Marty. He's always seen Marty as a loser, never wanting anything to do with him; but at least he's good at being a loser—he doesn't have to run around hiding in toilet stalls. He just found himself some zoned-out rats to dance to his piper's tune and goes around being their leader. That doesn't look as bad to Willie as it did three months ago. And Marty hit the nail on the head: Willie's a guy who's lost his best stuff. He limps to the kitchen door again—Jenny is still dancing—then back to lean against the counter. Marty and his friends don't know what to say, and almost none of them will look at him; except Marty, who says, "Hey, man, *you're* not in training. Want a beer?"

Willie automatically shakes his head, then, on impulse, nods. ". . . Sure. Why . . . not?"

There's an uneasiness as Willie drinks the beer. It doesn't taste good and nobody knows what to say to him, so he guzzles most of it. Marty's friends go back to their joint and their conversations and Willie slides off into his own head, staring at the stove; thinking about losing Jenny. He's startled to see Marty standing beside him with something in his hand. "Look, man," he says. "You look really bad. Take this. It'll make you feel better. You been through a lot; you oughta give yourself a break."

Willie pushes his hand away, anger welling up in him. "Six . . . months ago . . . wasted . . . you."

"Yeah, man. I know," Marty says, taking no offense. "Six months ago I wouldn't have offered. This is just something that could make you feel better. You look like hell, man."

Willie looks him in the eye. Again Marty looks sincere. Willie looks at the pill in Marty's hand. Marty puts it out. "You don't have to take it now," he says. "Save it for when you're really hurtin'."

He thinks of Jenny; thinks of where his life is headed; sees himself bumbling through the early-morning darkness in his jogging outfit. Who cares? He shrugs and takes the pill out of Marty's hand, drops it into his pocket and limps back to the living room.

Jenny stands behind him, massaging his neck and shoulders, which are always tight now; out of balance from compensating for his new body design. He feels the beer and closes his eyes, relaxed for the first time in months. Jenny's hands go to his head, work over his temples, lightly across his face, and he leans into them. He feels a deep sadness for how he's going to miss her when she gets tired of this new Willie; and his loneliness is bottomless. He wants to ask her what's going to happen; hear her say everything will be all right. But he knows better. Jenny whispers into his ear, "Gotta go to the bathroom. Don't move. I'll be right back."

As Jenny disappears through the kitchen, Willie reaches into his pocket, finds the pill Marty gave him among his keys and change, and pops it into his mouth.

Chronological time takes a vacation and there is only The Dream and variations on The Dream: The Dream that first revealed its ugly self sometime toward the end of Willie's coma. The scene is Promontory Point; they're driving the Golden Spike. Dignitaries in tall hats, railroad workers, a pile of railroad ties, a platform. Speeches. Chinese. Connecting east and west. Like in the history books, only Willie is a spectator. He's there; no hint it's a dream. The crowd gathers round, pinches closer as important men with no names or faces take turns driving the spike; like in the book. Then the crowd disappears. No one walks away; they simply dissolve, and Willie stares alone at the finished track. It's off. The right rail from the west connects to the left rail from the east, leaving the two outside rails to end in the dust. Willie knows it's him and his throat swells with panic; screams with no sound and falls to the dirt. When he looks up, he's on the mound at the Crazy Horse Electric game. Sal Whitworth sneers at him from the plate with Big Will's face. Willie fires the ball and in slow motion it adjusts itself to the middle of the plate, chest high to Sal Whitworth, who grins now; Willie's father's grin. The ball takes forever to get there; Sal roars and Willie hears the wind around the bat, but he's falling out of balance. There is the crack of the bat and the dull thud as the ball screams into the back of Willie's head. Sal circles the bases as the ball lies beside Willie sprawled near the mound. He screams at Willie and laughs. None of Willie's teammates move to field the ball; they laugh and point, too. Runners are produced from thin air at third and streak for home; Crazy Horse

Electric goes ahead by a hundred runs, maybe a thousand.

Now Willie is screaming on the couch. Jenny holds his head, calling for Johnny, who rushes from the kitchen. People turn to stare, riveted to their spots. Willie convulses, eyes rolled back, screaming from a bottomless pit. Jenny and Johnny yell his name, but he hears nothing; only bounces helplessly back and forth between Promontory Point, Utah, and the Crazy Horse Electric game; there is no relief.

Marty rushes in from the kitchen. "Oh, God," he says, "he's freakin'," and Johnny's head jerks up. "What?"

"Freakin' out," Marty says again. "I think he took some acid."

Johnny leaps from the couch to Marty's neck, throws him into a headlock and forces him to the ground, pounding his face with his free hand. Petey and two others try to pull him off, but Johnny throws them off like dolls, stands and kicks Marty hard in the stomach, then pulls him to his feet by the hair and runs him through the plate-glass window to the patio, where he leaves him bleeding.

Three guys hold Willie now, and Jenny cradles his head. His screams go on. Someone has fought through the craziness to call Emergency, and sirens wail through the quiet neighborhood, coming to take Willie away.

— CHAPTER 7 —

Willie sits in the small, darkened office just off the kitchen of the Community Center, nervously awaiting Cyril Wheat's arrival. Cyril Wheat, M.A. The state of Montana has funded a pilot program in which a therapist spends one day a week in each of five small towns, offering mental-health services to people referred by certain county, state or city agencies.

Willie notices the small rectangular sign tacked to the outside of the open door: WOULD YOU MIND IF I ASKED YOU TO TAKE YOUR SILLY-ASS PROBLEM DOWN THE HALL? *Not a bit,* Willie thinks. *A guy gets a little twisted out of shape and everybody decides he's crazy.* He looks at his watch; he'll give this Mr. Wheat, M.A., five more minutes. And he'll tell him right off; it wasn't *his* idea to see a shrink. Everything's under control now.

"Mr. Weaver, I presume." Willie's thoughts are broken by the appearance in the office doorway of a small-ish blond man with horn-rimmed glasses. He wears a light-colored T-shirt with something printed across the chest that Willie can't read because it's partially covered by his beige sport jacket, open down the front with the sleeves rolled up. His pants are old Levi cords and he wears running shoes with no socks. "I'm Cyril Wheat," the man says, and puts out his hand, then, noticing Willie is staring at his get-up, " 'Miami Vice.' "

Willie smiles. "Willie . . . Weaver," he says, shaking the therapist's hand.

Cyril whips out of his sport jacket, laying it across the desk, and Willie reads his shirt: GAY VEGETARIAN NAZIS

FOR JESUS. Cyril smiles and shrugs. "I'm a joiner," he says.

Willie's a little amused but still not at ease, so he sits quietly on the edge of his chair and waits while Cyril flips through the pile of manila folders on the desk. "Let's see," Cyril says, mostly to himself. "Ripper, Jack; no, that ain't you. Manson, Charlie; no, that ain't you either. Gotta be in here somewhere. Hitler, Adolf . . . Speck, Richard . . . Rogers, Roy . . . Boop, Betty . . . Ah, here it is; Weaver, William Jr." He opens the file and reads a minute. "Says here you think you're Napoleon Bonaparte . . . No, wait; it says Napoleon Pullapart."

Willie laughs a little and starts to speak, but Cyril is scribbling something on his notepad, speaking as he writes. "Client believes himself to be a cinnamon roll." He looks up again to Willie and shakes his head. "You're the first one of these I've had."

Willie shakes his head and smiles, looking at his knees. Cyril puts a hand on his shoulder and says gently, "But seriously now, folks . . ." and Willie eases back a little. Cyril flips again quickly through the information in the folder, closes it and plops it back onto the desk top. He's read it before. He says, "Rough time, eh?"

Willie shrugs. ". . . Sort of. I'm . . . better."

Cyril nods. "Well, let's start at the middle, then we can work both ways. Tell me about freaking out."

"You mean . . . at . . . the party?"

"At the party and afterward. Tell me everything you know about freaking out."

Willie describes, in his halting way, the feeling of pure lunacy that swept over him when the acid hit and how helpless he felt to stop it; how the horror took on a life of its own and smothered him; how he was transported out of Johnny's house to Hell and how it seemed like it would last forever. The telling is difficult, but never once does the therapist try to push or speak for him.

When he finally finishes, Cyril says, "Hoo-eee, that's some heavy shit."

"And . . . then . . . these dreams."

Cyril's hand shoots up, palm out. "Stop. I don't do dreams."

"I . . . thought . . . I was . . . supposed . . . to . . . talk about . . . everything."

Cyril stops a second and closes his eyes, thinking. "Oh, that's right," he says, "it's *windows* I don't do. Go ahead."

So Willie describes the tracks at Promontory Point that only partially meet and the murderous hardball ripping into the back of his skull off Sal Whitworth's bat; time and time and time again, until the anxiety and fear of the dream are matched by exhaustion.

"And what *really* happened?" Cyril asks.

Willie stares questioningly.

"In the game. What really happened?"

Tears fill Willie's eyes as he remembers the magical moment when he heard the crack of Sal's bat and, totally blind, *knew* where the ball would be; snatching it out of that tiny coordinate of time and space and speed. "It . . . wasn't . . . just . . . luck," he stammers. "I . . . knew . . . where the ball . . . was."

Cyril sits back, then says, as a statement of fact, "The game is a big deal to you."

Willie nods. Emptiness swells in him. He'd give anything to step back over that tiny sliver of time—the point of impact with the water ski—and be just a *hair* more cautious; back off the edge just enough. But the circumstances that allowed the Crazy Horse Electric game to be will never happen again, because he can't step back.

"Probably always will be a big deal," Cyril says. "That's the good news and the bad news."

Willie's insides are completely wrenched. He's glad in some way he came; glad he found a way to talk, and someone who would listen; but he wishes the time were up. There's no clock and he has no idea how long they've been there.

"So what other havoc has this wreaked in your life?" Cyril asks.

"What . . . about the . . . dreams?" Willie says. They've been haunting him for months now and he's not satisfied with just talking about them. He wants something; some information.

"Ah, the dreams are a cinch," Cyril says. "Even for a rookie like me. We'll talk about 'em in a minute. Give me the rest."

Willie talks about his father; his rage when he found out Willie had taken the acid; the side of his father he'd never seen before; an uncontrollable side. And about how his mother had tried to stand in and protect him, but didn't really have the power; how Willie thought he could see trouble in his parents' lives that he thought he'd probably had glimpses of when Missy died, but that only now seemed real. "I . . . feel . . . so guilty," he says. "I'm . . . not . . . a doper. I took . . . that . . . acid . . . because . . . I . . . don't know."

"You took that acid because it was there and because you were hurting about your girl. And your life."

Willie nods. "Stupid."

"It's a *mistake* if you do it once," Cyril says. "It's *stupid* if you do it again."

Willie smiles.

"So what else?"

Willie talks about the worst thing. "My dad . . .
won't . . . come . . . close . . . to me. There's . . .
something wrong. Something . . . I . . . don't . . .
know about. It . . . almost feels . . . like . . . he
. . . hates me. But . . . not . . . the acid. Before."

"Any guesses?"

Willie shakes his head.

"Well, pay attention to it. Maybe you'll come up with
something by next week. If you want your dad to come
in with you . . ."

Willie shakes his head again.

"Okay," Cyril says. "Anything else before we wrap it
up for the day?"

Willie dumps the last thing he's willing to let go of for
the day: that they're wanting to put him in Special Ed
classes at school; they think there's something wrong
with his brain. He says he's pretty sure he's as smart as
he ever was because he thinks the same, really, but he
just can't get it out.

"Did you tell them that?"

"What good . . . would . . . it . . . do? Look . . .
at . . . me. I . . . *look* brain-damaged." He goes on to
say he doesn't think he can make it in Special Ed classes;
that he just couldn't stand it.

"Special Ed, huh?" Cyril says.

Willie nods.

"A friend of mine and I were thinking about writing a
television series once. It was going to be about a talking
horse with an IQ of fifty. We were going to call it 'Special Ed.' "

Willie stares a second before he gets it, and laughs. "I
. . . have . . . a friend . . . you'd . . . like."

"Send him around. I could use the business." Cyril looks at his watch. "Uh-oh," he says. "Ran us right on past dinner. That's why they don't let me stay in one place with an office of my own. I can't get the hang of the fifty-minute hour. That's the most important thing you have to learn at counselor's school, you know. You have to learn to wrap everything up in fifty minutes. Then you can get a whole bunch of people in every day and become fabulously well-to-do. I didn't do well at counselor's school."

Willie stares at him, smiling and shaking his head.

"So," Cyril says. "I'll bet you're figuring, 'If this guy's a fer-real counselor, why the hell isn't he counseling?'"

Willie raises his eyebrows.

"That's a fair question." Cyril pushes his wooden chair onto its back legs and folds his arms. "I got no magic, Willie. If I did, I'd go on Carson. I can't make any of the things that have happened to you go away, but I might be able to find some ways to help you with them. First, don't take any more drugs."

"Don't . . . worry," Willie says. "I . . . may . . . *look* stupid . . ."

Cyril nods and goes on. "A lot of what happens now depends on truth. When you're afraid your girlfriend is going away or your friends are keeping you around just because they feel sorry for you, you have to *say* that to them. You have to do something with your life that doesn't set you up for that in the first place. If you present something for people to feel sorry for, they'll feel sorry for you. You have to set goals just like you always did and bust your ass going after them."

Right, Willie thinks. *I'll set goals. Let's see,* STOP DROOLING, *that could be one,* but he just looks at the counselor and nods.

"I know you think that's not possible right now," Cyril says, "but it is, and we can work on it. Now, if you're having trouble with your family, bring 'em in and we'll have some sessions together. If you want to have some sessions with your girlfriend, bring her in. Hell, bring in Sal Whitworth if you want to."

Willie smiles and nods. "The . . . dreams . . ."

"You're not gonna let me get out of here till I don my swami's hat, are you? Like I said, the dreams are easy. You dream better than most people talk. I would guess the tracks are just exactly what they appear to be. They don't come together, just like your system doesn't come together right now. That's your fear, and your dream just plays it out. And if you played the Crazy Horse Electric game again right now, the ball *would* hit you in the back of the head. You're not what you used to be, and you're resisting the hell out of it. Your dream is just telling you what you already know."

Willie looks disappointed.

"No magic, remember? But you can get a leg up on the dreams. Just tell yourself before you go to sleep that you already know that crap and you don't need to be reminded. Get it in your head that if you dream it, you're going to recognize it for what it is. That can take some of the power out."

That makes some sense to Willie. "Okay."

Cyril leans forward in the chair and the front legs come to the floor. He takes off his glasses and rests his elbows on his knees. "Willie, I have a feeling we're going to be seeing a lot of each other. What you're going through is a lot of loss. It's like death. You're feeling like something really important has died and you need to be able to mourn it; to grieve. Not many of us do that well. I think I can help with that."

Cyril's closeness, his offer of what seems like real compassion, embarrasses Willie a little, but it's also a powerful draw. He doesn't know how to respond.

Cyril winks at him. "So. I'll see you next week, right?"

Willie nods. "Right."

Cyril stands and gathers his folders off the desk, stuffing them into a pack sack behind his chair, then swings the sack around one shoulder. "One more thing," he says. "I know you've thought of suicide. You'd be crazy if you hadn't; then I'd *really* have my work cut out for me. I need to ask a favor."

"Yeah?"

"Yeah. If the idea gets serious, you call me, okay? If I were the best therapist in the world, they wouldn't have me out here in the backwater living out of a duffel bag. I don't think my professional reputation could handle losin' you right now; besides, I kind of like you, so don't you go makin' me look bad, okay? You get in trouble, you call me. Agreed?"

"Agreed," Willie says. He *has* thought of suicide. Seriously. And it's scary.

Out in the parking lot, as Willie limps toward his mother's car, he hears Cyril holler, "Willie, my boy!" and looks back.

"Them there school folks will put you in Special Ed over my dead body."

— CHAPTER 8 —

The whistle blows to call time and Willie is off the bench with his six-pack of Gatorade and a dry towel. The girls huddle around Coach Williams and Willie hands them the plastic bottles and offers the towel unobtrusively while the coach outlines the play she wants run—designed to get Jenny free on the wing for a last-second shot that will tie the game. Willie stands back from the huddle, across from where Jenny is concentrating on Coach Williams' every word. She's to cut off a screen on the left baseline, move diagonally across the key for the pass, and take the quick turnaround jumper from ten to twelve feet, a shot she must be eighty percent on tonight. The girls form a knot with their hands in the middle of the huddle, pump once with a loud "Let's do it!" and break. Willie's stomach dances with anticipation as the girls bring the ball in, and he's aware that something nagging down deep in him wants Jenny to blow it. He shakes the feeling away, murmuring, "Come on, Jen. Come on, Jen," under his breath. Jenny starts high and knifes in for the baseline as the ball comes in bounds, plants her foot and cuts back as Denise Caulder sets a perfect pick, scraping off Jenny's defender, who is on her like glue. Jenny takes the pass from the point guard on top with two seconds left, fakes right, spins left and lets loose a rainbow at the buzzer. She knows it's good as it leaves her fingertips and doesn't even watch it go in; simply turns and walks toward the bench as the crowd erupts. In overtime the girls walk away with it by eight points.

* * *

Willie lingers in the darkened locker room, picking up towels and gathering uniforms for washing, with only the light from the thirty-watt bulb above the manager's cage to illumine the room. The girls have showered and gone; Jenny waits just outside the door in the gym, making small talk with the school janitor, who patiently waits to lock up. Willie wishes he didn't know why he's stalling; why he can't go out there and congratulate Jen on a great game and just be with her. But he does know why.

"You gonna polish the lockers or what?" Jenny is standing at the door, silhouetted against the dim light in the gym, duffel bag hanging easily to her side.

"Be . . . right there," Willie says, and mumbles something about fixing a nozzle on the shower.

"So what did you think?" Jenny asks over a Coke at the Dragon. "Did we put 'em away or what?"

"You . . . put 'em . . . away," Willie says, nodding, hiding behind another long drink through his straw.

"So how about my shot at the end of regulation?" she ventures.

". . . Good . . . shot," Willie agrees. He takes another drink.

Jenny is quiet a fraction of a moment, considering. Then, "Good shot? It was a *great* shot! Two girls on me; I'da faked 'em out of their jocks if they had any. The ball left my fingers at the buzzer!" She leans forward. "Willie! Why can't I get anything from you? That was magic to me. There were a million things that could have gone wrong and none of them did. You're the only person I know who knows what that *feels* like."

Guilt flares in Willie's gut. Jenny wants something

from him and he's just too selfish and hurt to give it to her. "You're . . . right . . . Jen. It . . . was a . . . great . . . shot. Guess I'm . . . jealous."

Jenny sighs and sits back in the booth. "Yeah," she says. "Sorry."

Cyril Wheat sits forward in his chair and flips off his shoe, spreading his fourth and fifth toes to expose monumental cracking and peeling. Willie winces at the sight of it. "Amazing to me they can call this athlete's foot when it attacks the likes of me," Cyril says. "Nerd's foot, maybe. Or something Latin, like *pedus fungus dorcus.*" He reaches into his pack, extracting a metal spray can, and fires a powdery white stream at the afflicted area, breathing an audible sigh of relief. "Kills the offending digits," he says, as much to himself as to Willie. "Three or four days they fall off. You lose two shoe sizes, but a cure's a cure.

"So," he says, replacing the spray can in his pack, "you want to do some work on your girlfriend."

Willie nods. "She's . . . my . . . best friend," he starts. "She's . . . my . . . girlfriend . . . and she's . . . my . . . best friend."

Cyril nods. "Okay."

"I'm . . . *mad* . . . at her . . . all . . . the time. Sometimes . . . I feel . . . like I . . . *hate* her."

"Sounds like my marriage," Cyril says. "What do you hate her about?"

Willie shrugs, then the look of recognition crosses his face and he says, "Sports. School. All . . . the things . . . she . . . can do. Sometimes . . . I just . . . hate her . . . for it."

Cyril's nodding again. "She's getting all the stuff you used to get, right? And she wants to share it with you like you used to with her, right? And that would be okay with you if you were still getting it, but now it just taps into what you've lost and you get angry at yourself and angry at her and angry at the world, right?"

Willie feels as if Cyril's been reading his mail. "So . . . what do . . . I . . . do?"

"Welcome to ABC's Wide World of Changes, Willie. The only thing you can do is let that go. That golden boy isn't you anymore, and as long as you keep measuring yourself up against him, you're gonna be mad as hell at *everybody*. And I'll guarantee another thing. Keep it up and you'll lose your girl." Cyril's eyes are watery; he's feeling Willie's pain; but he's dead-on straight with him. "We've been seeing each other for a couple of months now, Willie, and you've worked through some pretty tough stuff, but if you don't find a way to get your head straight about this, it'll all be for nothing." He sits back. "And you'll lose your girl." They've been over this before. Cyril has spent the last sixty days letting Willie find his own answers; now he's supplying some of his own.

Willie nods and tells him the scary part is that when he's feeling that way, he *wants* to lose his girl.

"Well, keep it up and you'll get your wish. If I were you, I'd talk about this with Jenny. Bring her in here if you have to, but talk about it with her. No way she'll understand it if you don't. By the way, I like your shirt."

Willie's wearing a gray short-sleeved sweatshirt with LURCH stenciled across the front—his attempt at attacking his problem head-on with humor; that came out of session number three. He has another at home just like it, except it says QUASIMODO.

He decides to ask Jenny if she'll come in with him next week.

* * *

Willie lies in bed sometime after midnight thinking how his world is coming apart. Every time he gains a victory, there's nothing to it. He won the battle to keep himself out of Special Ed, but so what? He still feels like a creep every time he stumbles into class or has to fight through the obstacle course between his brain and his mouth to answer even a simple question. He got back into sports, as much as he could, by taking the manager's spot on the girls' basketball team. Big deal. All it does is remind him that he couldn't take the worst girl on the team one-on-one. Every time he stands up in front of the crowd to give the girls water or pass around the towel, he feels like a circus freak, as if every eye in the place were trained on him, pitying him; or laughing, depending on how he sees it that day.

And then there's his parents. There are no victories with his parents; only distance. Distance between him and them and distance between them. His mom has grown tired of Willie's frustration and rage when his physical world won't cooperate, so she lectures; his dad ignores it. Cavernous silences hold them hostage at the dinner table. After dinner the television set is never off, a safe focus for everyone's attention. But there is no way to address *any* of this because everyone is so polite, as if presenting graciousness will stamp out the reality. Willie has thought about trying to get his parents to go with him to see Cyril, but he fears that bringing it up will serve only to light the fuse to the bundle of dynamite destined to blow his family into the cosmos.

Jenny's horn blasts through the cold, clear early-morning air as Willie takes his last bite of toast and gulps down his orange juice. He's dog tired from lying awake all night wondering if things would balance out for his folks if he disappeared from this equation. Could they pull it back together if they didn't have him around to remind them of every damn thing that's wrong in their lives?

He slumps into the shotgun seat beside Jenny and stares out the window, saying only, ". . . Tired," when she asks what's wrong. He'd like to tell her what he's been thinking, and there was a time not too long ago when he would have; when he would have shared any secret. But the guilt—almost panic—he feels about their relationship tells him it couldn't stand the stress. Jen would tell him he's thinking crazy; she would get Johnny to say it, too, and probably a bunch of the others; but no one who really knows the situation can deny it: If Willie Weaver were gone, his parents' lives would be better.

"Check this out," Big Will says after work, hanging his coat on the wooden coat rack in the hall and holding out a red-and-white plastic sack from Brinson's Sporting Goods. "Your new sport." He hands the sack to Willie and waits expectantly as Willie reaches in and feels the cool leather grip of the racquet; wraps the fingers of his good hand around it and extracts it from the bag.

"Racquetball?" he says. It isn't really a question.

"Racquetball," Big Will replies. "It's made for you. You only use one hand in racquetball, it's a relatively small court and it takes as much smarts as physical skill. I have a court reserved over at the club for seven-thirty tonight. Got a rule book right here. This is the beginning of a new career for you. We'll take our time; learn it slow. Don't even have to tell anyone until you have the hang of it."

Willie has mixed feelings. He knows how to play racquetball; he played a couple of times before he was hurt. And he wasn't bad. The idea of a sport that will focus on his good side instead of his bad makes sense, but it's hard to imagine he'll ever be good at any sport and he feels like he might be setting himself up for another failure. He's agreed with Cyril that he needs to make smart choices, but the reality here is there's no going against Big Will when his mind is made up; never has been. You just don't say no to Willie's dad before you've tried. Besides, Big Will sounds kind of excited, and it's the first attempt he's made since the accident, and particularly since the drug incident at Johnny's, to get close to Willie again.

Willie stuffs his clothes into a basket and removes his gym shorts and sweatshirt from his workout bag. Without comment, Big Will reaches over and turns the LURCH sweatshirt inside out before Willie puts it on. "No more Lurch," he says. "No more Quasimodo. You're on your way back."

Willie thinks, *Sure, Dad,* but only nods. "No . . . more . . . Lurch," he says with a partial smile.

On the court Big Will says, "We won't play a game tonight, just work on skills. I'll give you stuff right down the middle off the front wall at first, and you just get it back to the front wall. Nothing fancy. Gotta take it at a pace that works." He bounces the ball once and takes an easy shot. Willie goes for it and overextends, hitting the ball with the racquet handle, but it does sail weakly to the front wall and his dad puts it right down the middle again. This time Willie lunges forward and the ball strikes the edge of the racquet, shooting straight up to the ceiling and straight back down.

"Don't get overanxious," Big Will says, seeing Willie's frustration as he grips the racquet handle tighter. "This is just like any other *ball* game. You have to watch the ball at all times."

Willie settles down a little, but he can't get used to his body; hauling his left side around is like dragging small sacks of concrete, and it distracts him from his concentration on the ball. The frustration is tremendous already, but his dad's calmness allows him more patience. He works at just getting to the ball; looking ahead to where it's going to be so he can get a jump on it; but eighty percent of his shots go awry because he has to *tell* the different parts of his body what to do instead of letting them act on their own, like they used to. After twenty minutes he can feel his dad starting to get tense.

"Want to . . . stop?" Willie asks. "We could . . . come . . . back."

Big Will shakes his head. "Can't quit," he says. "Let's just stay with it awhile; let you get the hang of it." There's an edge on his voice, and Willie works harder getting to the ball, hoping to show his dad immediate improvement. But the harder he tries, the more mistakes he makes. He lunges for a shot that's almost out of reach, catches it hard in the middle of the webbing, but with no control, and drives it high off the front wall into a long arc that carries it over the open back wall, over the spectators' walkway and into the court behind them.

Big Will throws his racquet down in disgust. "God damn it, Willie, pay attention! Concentrate! Watch the ball! Damn it, you look like a girl out here!" He catches himself, immediately reining in his anger; pinches the bridge of his nose, closing his eyes. "Forget it," he says through partially clenched teeth. "I'm sorry. I shouldn't have said that." He walks out the back door to retrieve the ball.

"You don't look like a girl," Big Will says on his return, placing his big hand easily on Willie's shoulder. "That's just my frustration. I'm sorry." He breathes deep.

"We . . . can . . . stop," Willie says. "Come back . . . tomorrow."

Big Will shakes his head again. "No. Can't leave the court on a bad shot. Now just take your time and concentrate. Keep your eye on the ball. We'll get ten good hits and go."

Willie relaxes and the next two shots are good ones. Encouraged, Big Will keeps them coming right down the middle. Willie gets a good third shot, then a fourth. But the next one shoots straight up off the handle and the sixth he drives into the floor. Big Will slows them up a little to let him get his bearings back, but Willie's lost it. He stumbles, or gets to the ball too late, or too soon. Pretty soon he can't see the ball through the tears of frustration.

Big Will says not a word, just keeps hitting the ball off the front wall, at first easy, then harder and harder as he sees it doesn't matter, that Willie can't hit anything anyway. Big Will is silently furious. Finally, as Willie reaches for a backhand that careens off the side wall and dies in the middle of the floor, Big Will slips his hand out of the safety string and fires his racquet sidearm at the front wall. It pops like a gunshot, then lies twisted on the floor. "Just get out of here," he says. "Let's just get out of here. If you're not going to try, there's no point to it."

"I'm . . . trying," Willie says.

"You're *not* trying. You were hitting the ball fine; then

you gave up. You want to be a cripple all your life, just keep it up. When it gets a little tough, slack off."

Tears stream down Willie's face as he slips his hand out of the safety string and limps toward the door.

"You just going to leave the ball there?" his dad asks, and Willie slowly retraces his steps to retrieve the ball lying by the front wall. As he leans over to pick it up, he catches movement out of the corner of his eye and glances up to see someone watching from the walkway between courts. He's overwhelmed by the sight of all this through someone else's eyes and he falls back against the side wall and sinks to the floor, dropping his head between his knees, sobbing.

Big Will is in control of himself again and guilt washes over him in a wave. "Come on, son," he says. "Get up. That's me, not you. I'm really sorry. I should have let you quit when you were doing well. We'll do it differently next time."

But Willie knows it is him. His dad isn't the cripple. His dad isn't some stupid jerk lurching and lunging around the racquetball court in a body that doesn't even belong to him. His dad isn't the one who's going to lose his girl, who has to see a shrink every week because he's too big a baby to handle what life passes out. It is Willie. It's *his* life. And he's stuck in it.

Big Will slides his hand gently under Willie's armpit and helps him to his feet and, with his other hand in the middle of Willie's back, guides him toward the locker room.

— CHAPTER 9 —

Cyril encouraged the Weavers' family doctor to pre-
scribe some pills for nights like this, but Willie resists
taking them as long as he possibly can because of the
way he feels when he wakes up in the morning. "Yeah,
they can zone ya," was Cyril's response to Willie's com-
plaint. "Most drugs have a down side, whether you get
them on the street or from a doctor."

So tonight Willie lies in bed holding off a few minutes
more, a few minutes more, hoping he'll drop off on his
own and not have to face negotiating the icy streets in a
borderless haze on his morning run. He and his dad
came directly home from the racquetball courts in a
miserable silence and Willie went directly to bed. His
dad tried to apologize once again, and Willie openly
accepted it, but the gap would not be closed tonight.
The echo of the hard rubber ball whapping into the
wood, the sound of the racquet careening off the side
wall, the ghastly uneven cadence of it all ring in Willie's
ears, making sleep impossible. At three he slides out of
bed, wraps himself in his bathrobe and carefully feels
his way down the stairs to the kitchen for something to
eat.

Warm milk helps sometimes, and he searches through
the food cupboard for some instant chocolate to go in it;
something to keep it from tasting like it just came out of
the cow. As he pours the milk into the pan, he hears
voices from his parents' room and quietly moves to the
kitchen door to see if he can hear them better. Unable
to make out any specific words, he pads back through

the kitchen and turns on the hot plate. Now the voices are louder and he thinks he hears his name, so he creeps back through the kitchen, across the living room to their bedroom door, thinking how strange it is for them to be awake this late. Sandy has been known to get up occasionally through the night, but Will Sr. sleeps like a log from the moment his head hits the pillow until his alarm blasts him loose around five-thirty.

Willie puts his ear to the door and listens.

". . . to excel at that sport or any other. No right at all. Leave him alone. God, do you know what he must feel like? Let *him* decide what he wants to play."

Big Will sounds low; even embarrassed. "I know, I know. I shouldn't push him, but sometimes I think if I don't he won't do anything. He'll just hide out."

"Then let him hide out," she says. "He'll come out of it eventually."

"Do you *know* that?"

"I know if you keep pushing, when he does come out there won't be anyone to come *to*."

"Jesus, Sandy. He took *drugs*. He took *acid*. Kids start playing around with that stuff and they don't come out of *anything*."

"He *told* us what that was about, Will. He's not going to take drugs again."

Willie is uncomfortable listening in; respecting privacy is a family rule. But he needs to know . . .

"A lot of parents say that, Sandy," Will says. "Willie's got every reason in the world to want to escape."

Almost inaudibly, Sandy says, "You mean *you* do."

Big Will is instantly angry. "What do you mean by that?"

There's a pause. "I mean sometimes I think this has

been harder on you than on Willie. I hate to say this, Will, but there are times you act ashamed of Willie. And he feels it, too; I can sense it. How do you think he felt at the racquetball courts tonight?"

"I'm *not* ashamed of him! What the hell's the matter with you, Sandy?"

Now their voices are filling the house and Willie backs away from the door, moves over toward the stairs; sits.

"What's the matter with me? I'll tell you what's the matter with me. I'm so angry at you I could scream. I could leave. When Missy died, you were *so* righteous. You were so goddam righteous. You sat around telling us all how we shouldn't blame ourselves; you even got irritated with me when I couldn't stop saying how guilty I felt. 'Stick together,' you said. 'Look at the good things,' you said. You were *so* strong. You were so goddam *good.* You didn't have to feel bad. Hell, you weren't even around. Couldn't be Will Weaver's fault. He was at work."

Sandy takes a shaky breath, and Willie realizes she's almost out of control. But she's not slowing down a second. "So now something happens that puts a crick in your world. *Your* kid; the one who was supposed to grow up and go to the goddam Rose Bowl; *your* kid gets put out of commission. I want to know where your strength is now, Will Weaver. How come you're not so *good* now?"

There's silence, and Willie can't imagine what's on his father's face this minute.

Sandy continues. "Will, this family is coming apart at the seams. Since the day Willie got hurt, it's just been coming apart at the seams. And you're the reason. You don't talk to anybody, you don't help out; you don't give anyone any reason to believe that things will ever be any better. And I'm about full up."

"That your solution?" Big Will says, his low voice vibrating with tension. "Things get a little tough and you hit the road."

Sandy explodes. "A little tough! A little tough! Don't you put this back on me, Will Weaver. *I* don't bury my head in the newspaper night after night and pretend my family doesn't exist! I don't treat our son like a leper; or worse yet, like he's invisible. He's not some possession, you know. He's not a car you can take back to the dealer because it doesn't run right. He's our son. And you're the one he's closest to and you better learn to be decent. *You* drove the boat, Will. Just like I chattered away across the street when Missy died."

"Yeah, well, you're off the hook!" Big Will yells, his restraint crumbled. "You don't have to sit around and look at your screw-up every day. Missy's six feet under. She's a memory. Willie's stumbling around in front of me from before sunrise to long after sunset, just reminding me. You know why he was without air so long? Because I panicked. Because I almost smothered him trying to get that damn jacket off. If it hadn't been for Jenny, I'd have drowned him. And I'm not so sure that wouldn't have been better. Let the little shit off the hook!"

"Let *you* off the hook, you mean! Grow up, Will. Just grow the hell up. Get real. Life isn't just the Rose Bowl."

Willie's eyes are glued to the closed bedroom door. Smoke from the scalded milk drifts off the stove, bringing him back. He slips into the kitchen to switch off the hot plate, pour the milk into the sink; then slinks back upstairs to the strains of his parents' relentless accusations. He's never heard them fight before, much less aim every shot below the belt. Devastated, he crawls back into bed and pulls the covers over his head.

He just wants out.

Willie limps down the center of the hall, staring at a spot above the archway leading to the stairwell, letting the other students dodge him for a change. He's taking stock, like Cyril taught him. Counting the positives, over and over. There aren't many, after last night. There's Jenny; in a session with Cyril, she promised she'd hang in there with him; promised she'd stay. And there's Johnny; he's a good friend sometimes, though he can be a pain in the butt trying to help. His speech is getting better and lately he's been feeling like maybe he's going to get it under control. That's it, though. His parents . . . no, not supposed to think about that. Just the positives. His mind moves back to Jenny, then Johnny, his speech . . .

"Got a new sport for you." Johnny's voice breaks his concentration as Johnny rushes to catch him, then slows to match Willie's pace. "It's perfect. Racquetball," he says, pulling a shiny new racquet from behind his back. "You only need one hand. Small court. Perfect for you. My dad took me over to play the other night. We can give it a try any time you're ready."

Willie looks at him and can only smile. "Don't . . . think so," he says. "Don't . . . think I . . . could . . . get . . . into it."

Just before noon, Willie follows the enclosed walkway connecting the main building to the gymnasium. He's on his way to tell Coach Williams he doesn't think it's working out too well for him managing the girls' basketball team. He's spent the whole morning concentrating, and the positive aspects of his life are worn thin. His parents' fight rings in his ears and he can't force the feelings out any longer. He just feels too awful to pretend he can be around athletes of any kind when he can't be one, too. *Let the little shit off the hook. Let you off the hook, you mean.* The voices are real. *He's not some car you can take back to the dealer because it doesn't run right . . . doesn't run right . . . doesn't run right.*

"Oh, hi, Willie." He looks up, startled, to see Jenny and Jeff Rhodes entering the walkway through the side door, from outside.

"Hi," he says quickly, realizing instantly something's wrong. He looks into Jenny's eyes, then Jeff's. Jeff darts a look at him, then to the wall behind his head. "Hi . . . Jeff."

"Hey, Willie. How you doin'?" Jeff says. He glances quickly at Jenny, then back to the wall. "Look," he says, "I gotta get to class. I'll see you guys later."

Jenny's recovered. "Okay, Jeff. Take it easy. Tell Debbie I'll catch up with her in Algebra."

Debbie is Jeff's girlfriend.

Supposedly.

Jenny turns to Willie; touches his arm. "Where're you headed?" she asks.

"Out . . . to see . . . Coach Williams."

"How come?"

"Just gotta . . . talk to her . . . for . . . a minute."

"Want some company?"

Willie shakes his head. "No. That's . . . okay. Got some . . . other stuff . . . to do."

Jenny smiles and pecks his cheek. "Okay. I'll see you at lunch."

Thoughts of his parents' fight wash out of his head like

water draining out of a bathtub, replaced by the flash across Jeff's and Jenny's faces. In the months since the accident Willie has developed radar for hidden meaning; unspoken language. It's as real to him as anything he can touch or feel. But Jenny wouldn't do that. She's a friend. She was a friend before all this; a good one. She said she wouldn't do that; she'd hang in. Certainly there are times when his intuition is wrong. Cyril *said* there will be times when he's particularly paranoid. On the other hand, no one ever tells him anything. Friends are so careful, there's no way he can trust them. Petey is the only one. Words tumble out of his mouth long before he might even think of censoring them. Everyone else is on guard. Willie feels himself physically pushing his stomach back down where it belongs. Whether he's right or wrong about Rhodes and Jenny, there's no way to find out. And Rhodes is a class guy. Pretty good athlete. Great student. Funny. Good-looking. Willie feels the black cloud of his worst fear taking shape.

With a deep breath he continues out to resign his position as flunky for girls' roundball.

He skips lunch because he knows he can't play it straight with Jenny. If she has been seeing Rhodes, she'll know he senses something and it will be awful. If she hasn't, she'll dig out of Willie what's bothering him and he'll feel like a fool. He pulls on his coat and snow boots and wanders aimlessly for the lunch period through the neighborhood surrounding the school. If he could *just stop the unraveling;* finally get to the last of the awful pain seemingly caused by his mere presence. Hell, he knew Jenny was going to go. He's been saying it all along; but holding a little back, really; holding on to a small spot deep down that said maybe Jenny was superhuman. But he knows that "uh-oh" look Rhodes gave her in the walkway.

He slips quietly into his desk minutes after the start of Algebra, purposely late to avoid a conversation with Jenny. He lays his cane on the floor parallel to the desks beside the rest of his books, brings out his notebook and starts his hand-held tape recorder; Cyril's "equalizer" for Willie's slowness. Actually he doesn't need the cane anymore, but he carries it sometimes because some of the guys on the ball team had it made special. The head is a gold baseball inscribed: WILLIE WEAVER—1, CRAZY HORSE ELECTRIC—0. Petey's idea.

Petey hustles into class five minutes late, apologizing to Mr. Zimmer as he comes through the door about having run an errand for the Journalism class.

Mr. Zimmer nods patiently as Petey babbles on, then finally says, "Mr. Shropshire, do me a favor, okay? When you come in late, come in mute," and Petey nods and keeps right on explaining, rounding the corner by Willie's desk, kicking the cane the length of the aisle, tripping in the process, turning to save himself on Willie's desk. He catches Willie's tape recorder with the side of his arm and it crashes to the ground. In an instant Petey retrieves the cane and rushes back to pick up the damaged recorder, apologizing all the while to Willie, whose hands cover his ears, and whose eyes are closed.

"God, Willie," Petey says, "I'm really sorry. I didn't mean to mess up your stuff." He tries to hand him the cane and, when Willie doesn't respond, leans it against his desk, placing the recorder carefully on Willie's book. "Really, Willie. It was an accident." He reads Willie's pulling away as anger at his clumsiness when all Willie really wants is for the attention to shift elsewhere. "Is it okay, man?" Petey says. "I don't think your tape recorder's broken . . ."

"Stop . . . it!" Willie screams. "Stop it! Get . . . away from me. Everybody get . . . away . . . from me! The . . . next . . . person apologizes . . . to me . . . for . . . anything . . . I'll . . . hit 'em in the head!" He picks up the cane in his right hand and swings it in front of him. "I'll . . . hit 'em. I . . . will. I'll . . . hit 'em . . . right . . . in the head!"

Petey is struck dumb, staring at Willie from his seat on the floor two feet away from the end of the cane. "I'm sorry . . ." he starts, and Willie swings. "Shut up!" he screams; Petey is silent.

Mr. Zimmer is standing at his desk, but hasn't spoken, nor moved.

Willie points the baseball end of the cane at Jeff Rhodes, starts to speak, then turns to Jenny. "You lied . . . Jenny. I . . . saw it . . . today. I know," though he didn't really, not until this moment when Jenny glances to Jeff, back to Willie, then drops her gaze to the floor.

A guttural roar starts in Willie's gut, spraying out through clenched teeth, as he fires his cane through the closed window out into the snow. He snatches his books and starts for the door as Mr. Zimmer, speaking softly, carefully, tries to bring him down. "Willie . . ."

Willie looks him square in the eye and says, ". . . Don't. I'm . . . leaving. I'll . . . pay . . . for . . . the window." Then he's gone.

Jenny catches him in the hall, headed for the steps. "Wait, Willie. I'm sorry. I didn't know what to do."

"You . . . coulda . . . just . . . told me . . . the . . . truth," Willie says between clenched teeth. "Just . . . the truth."

"I couldn't. I just couldn't say it."

"You . . . said . . . you'd stay." Somewhere deep in him, Willie knows he'll be sorry; that he's ready to say things that are irreversible, but he can't stop.

"Willie . . ."

"No . . . 'Willie.' Just . . . stay away . . . from . . . me. You . . . lied. I . . . hate you . . . Jenny."

And now Jenny is wounded. "You hate me! You hate me! I saved your life, you bastard. You don't even know that. Your dad was sure a lot of help . . . And what do you think it's been like for the last six months with you walking around like a goddam zombie? There's no sense of humor. There's no fun. You treat your friends like spit. I'd have stayed with you, Willie, if you'd have made any attempt to be decent. But no! Not Willie Weaver! If he can't be a hero, then to hell with everyone else . . ."

Stunned, Willie stares into her eyes. He just wants to hurt her back. "You . . . bitch. You . . . lied."

Jenny wheels to go. "To hell with you, Willie. I can't spend the rest of my life feeling sorry for you. To hell with you."

Willie stumbles through his own tears down the stairs to the front door and kicks the panic bar with his good foot, blasting the door open against the outside wall. For a reason he doesn't understand, he stops to retrieve his cane, leaving his books lying in the deep snow. Then he jerks and lurches for home.

— CHAPTER 10 —

The big tires of the Greyhound hum on the cold, dry pavement, headed west. Willie stares out over the shadowy land, cast in an eerie blue by the near-full moon reflecting off the snow. The bus driver could shut down the headlights if he wanted to. Willie switches positions uncomfortably, pulling his coat tighter to his chin, pressing the button on the side of the arm rest, allowing the seat to recline a few inches. Outside, the snowbanks shoot by like walls on a bobsled run, interrupted only by tall, bare willows; markers placed there to signal state crews where to plow when the road and the bank and the sky all blend together.

His ticket is for Spokane, but he'll get another one at the bus station there and head south. California, maybe. There are distant relatives outside of San Francisco, he thinks, and some kids he met at a West Coast All-Star game when he played Babe Ruth League. Worse comes to worst, he'll look one of them up. He can't remember exactly where most of them are from, but it can't be too hard to find them once he's there.

He sure couldn't stay in Coho.

Willie stole from his parents before he left; went through every nook and cranny in the house looking for money. He cleaned out his savings account: $479. Told Millie at the teller's window he was buying a VCR.

Millie thought that would be a wise purchase.

At the drugstore which doubles as the bus station, he told Al Carson he was headed for Spokane to see some kind of specialist. Al didn't bat an eye.

Willie didn't leave a note. If his parents knew he was actually leaving, they'd check the bus station and Amtrak and if they found out which way he headed, they could have him picked up in Spokane. *Crippled kid*, he hears them describing him. *Got a cane with a brass baseball on the handle.*

No way. He'll write later; a postcard from Spokane maybe, saying he's headed for Seattle. Gotta do this right. Gotta disappear right; take appropriate evasive action. First thing he's done right since the accident.

Willie stares out the window onto the infinite snow-fields and the tears stream once again; they just won't stop. He hopes he can pull it together in Spokane so the ticket man won't be suspicious; but there are many miles to go before he has to worry about that, so for now he lets them run.

The woman beside him stinks. She's old and she stinks. She's got her wrinkled old self wrapped in a frayed, colorless afghan; her nose whistles incessantly, and Willie tries to block out her fragile, sickly sounds. Still, it's better than sitting beside someone who wants to talk.

Outside, the ocean of snow shoots past.

In the Spokane terminal, it turns out, there's nothing to worry about. No one there, nor in any other bus terminal on the route, cares one bit about a crippled kid with a Crazy Horse baseball cane. Probably Willie's parents think he's at one of his friends' and are only really worried that they'll have to explain last night's fight to him. That is, if they've figured out he heard it. He's traveling under the name Louie Banks, after a character in a book he likes, to be sure they can't trace him, and at the counter in Spokane he's without his cane. He says only "San Francisco" and answers all other questions with head movement so no one will remember a kid who couldn't talk right.

Shooting through the early-morning blackness of the eastern Washington scabland, headed for Portland, then south, he feels a huge blanket of anonymity covering his tracks; a frontier scout, pursued by the Sioux, but he's riding his getaway horse down the middle of the creek. Only the best could track him.

And Willie's mom and dad aren't at their best right now.

Each leg of the trip takes forever. The Greyhound is like a huge pencil; the land an enormous children's game of Connect-the-Dots. The Greyhound pencil connects *all* the dots, stopping at each, if even for only a few seconds.

At approximately forty-five-minute intervals, a choking fear creeps in, almost paralyzing Willie, telling him to turn back before he's in so deep there's no way out. But each time he looks at what he'd be turning back *to,* he strengthens his resolve. He'd rather be dead than be the person he is in his parents' and his friends' lives.

He held on to his rage at Jenny for only a few hundred miles; then it began to melt and now he remembers their friendship. But the searing pain of seeing her with Rhodes, of *knowing,* doesn't dissipate quite so easily. He's not mad anymore, though, and he wishes he hadn't called her a bitch. He'll write someday; apologize for that.

And Johnny. Boy, he's going to miss Johnny. All those crazy jokes; his lunatic way of walking the very edge of people's tolerance, yet knowing that edge as well as a tightrope artist knows his wire. And Johnny was the only one who showed any signs of understanding; of knowing Willie didn't want to be babied or looked out for. Johnny just didn't know what to do with that. *He might have, though,* Willie thinks, *given a little more time.*

Boy, he's going to miss Johnny.

In the Portland terminal, waiting for the connecting bus down the coast, Willie thinks of Cyril. Cyril would chide him for running away—for not facing everything hurtling his way. But Cyril is a friend and he'll understand, at least. He'll talk to Willie's parents and to his friends and piece things together. He'll understand. Just the same, it would be good to drop him a line.

In the tiny gift shop, he buys several plain postcards, stands at an eating counter and scribbles:

> *I'm okay. Can't make it there, though. Hope you understand.*
>
> *Willie*

on four of them, then waits by the ticket counter near a sign reading PHOENIX until a boy about his age approaches to buy a ticket. Willie watches the boy, reads his face, looking for something he can trust. Finally, as the boy moves away from the counter, Willie approaches him, asking, in his halting way, if the boy would do him a favor and mail these postcards from Phoenix. "It's . . . a joke," he says, only half smiling. "But . . . it's . . . real im . . . portant." The boy looks doubtful, hesitates a second, and Willie says, "It's . . . worth . . . five bucks."

The boy looks poor. Patches on his pants, a shirt too big; probably his dad's or an older brother's. Five bucks would be nice. "Okay," he says, and takes the postcards, placing them carefully in an outside pocket of his tattered duffel bag and depositing the five-dollar bill in the watch pocket of his Levi's.

Willie hears the call over the intercom and heads for his bus. He says, "Thanks."

— CHAPTER 11 —

In the Oakland bus terminal, Willie sits back in his seat and waits. The driver has said there'll be a delay before the bus crosses the Bay Bridge to San Francisco, and Willie is in no hurry to get off. The bus has become something of a cocoon, another cave, and he's aware that once he steps off for good, he's out in the open. On his own. He pictures finding a motel room for a few days, or a hotel, and looking for work; maybe at a McDonald's or a Kentucky Fried Chicken, something that will keep him from having to spend all his money while he figures out what to do next.

Doubts crowd into his thinking and he forces them out. They persist: *You should have gone somewhere you know someone. Who's going to hire a cripple? Who's going to hire someone who can't even tell them what he wants?* No. He'll just walk up, *take his time* and tell them what he wants. His speech is better; he knows that. As long as he's not nervous . . .

His thoughts shatter at the sound of the bus driver's voice over the intercom: "Ladies and gentlemen, we're going to have to make some minor repairs on this bus before we can take her into San Francisco. If we can't get them done in a half-hour or less, we'll transfer you to a different vehicle. If you're in a hurry, we can issue you a transfer to the local bus transit system or to BART. Those transfers can be picked up in the terminal at the main desk. Thank you for your patience."

There are groans; passengers talk among themselves; a few pull their baggage down from above and move out of the bus and toward the terminal. For a moment Willie is relieved. It gives him more time to think; time to fend off this strange new world he's chosen. He can sit here while they fix the bus and nothing will change. But it's getting late; after ten. Dark. He better check things out. As he stands, his bad leg fails him momentarily and he catches himself on the back of the seat in front of him, waiting to feel his balance, then reaches for his duffel bag in the top rack. And the cane. The driver is writing something on a clipboard and Willie stops momentarily, waiting for his attention. The driver looks up, only semi-patient.

"Excuse . . . me," Willie says. "What's . . . BART?"

The driver seems momentarily confused; then a flash of recognition as he realizes what Willie is asking. "Bay Area Rapid Transit," he says. "It's like a subway. You can take a city bus to the BART station. It goes under the bay to San Francisco."

Willie nods. "Thanks." He starts to walk away.

"Someone picking you up?" the driver asks.

Willie's not sure how to answer. He doesn't want to seem lost; can't flounder. "Not here," he says finally. "In San Francisco."

The driver nods, maybe not quite believing him. "Well," he says, "you might do well to wait for the bus to be repaired. This isn't the best part of town to be out on the street alone; even to catch the bus. Especially for a . . . For a kid."

For a cripple, Willie thinks. *Just say it, for Christ's sake.* He says, "Thanks," then moves slowly through the concrete garage, the sound of his cane echoing off the bare gray walls, into the brightly lit terminal.

The Oakland bus terminal is not what Willie Weaver had in mind when he got it in his head to travel. Though a janitor moves constantly with a mop, the floors are sticky and grimy. Transients sleep on nearly half the available benches; men and women whose dignity has been swallowed up by their histories; histories a relatively sheltered young man from Coho, Montana, can only imagine. These are not the indigents who pass through his hometown, receiving traveler's aid or help from the Red Cross to get to the next small town; and these are not farmers or ranchers down on their luck, looking for extended credit to get through the winter or through a dry spell. These are people to whom hard times—desperate times—are the order of the day. "Abandon Hope . . ." is written across their faces in greasy city dirt.

Willie is astonished by what he sees, and immediately decides to march right over to the ticket counter and purchase a ticket back home. But his parents' voices echo through his head from the bedroom, followed instantly by the poster-sized, full-color paste-up of Jenny and Rhodes bursting into the walkway together. The answer, Willie decides, isn't to turn tail and run. The answer is to get the hell out of the Oakland bus station.

Willie moves to the rear of the line of people waiting for Alameda County Transit and BART transfers and stands patiently as those ahead of him receive instructions. He strains his ears to hear; to get a picture of what he'll need to do when he gets outside. There's a bus stop down the block, he hears the man behind the counter saying, and the 51 bus will take you to BART. If you miss the 51, just wait for any bus with the BART logo. Or you can walk the several blocks to the downtown station; might be faster, depending on how the buses are running. Willie decides he'll do that; the fewer transfers he has to make, the better chance he has of reaching the destination. Getting on local transportation has the feeling of getting on the Space Shuttle. He asks for, and gets, instructions to the nearest BART station, takes the BART transfer from the ticket man and heads for the door.

Willie wasn't paying attention when the Greyhound pulled into the terminal; he was half asleep, slumped down in his seat with his coat most of the way over his head, so he had no idea what part of town he was in. In Coho the bus station is also the local drugstore; certainly as safe a place as there is in town. But the Oakland bus terminal is not in the center of some innocuous middle-class community. The Oakland bus terminal is *downtown*, and Willie steps into an almost suffocating wall of tension as he moves out onto the street. There are predators here. Though the area directly in front of the terminal is brightly lit, he can barely see to the end of the block in either direction through the darkness. Bars cover the windows of all the buildings adjacent to the terminal, and for as far as he can see, for that matter. Bums huddle against vacant buildings, coats pulled high, hats pulled low; insulating themselves like ostriches from the reality surrounding them. The sense of danger is so thick, so real, it permeates Willie's heavy jacket, and though the temperature is in the high fifties —warmth he hasn't felt since before October—he shivers. He turns back into the terminal; he'll get the bus transfer and not try to walk to BART, knowing he'd be frozen with fear by the time he got to the end of the block. The line is longer than before, but he waits, scooting his bag forward with his cane each time another customer is serviced.

"Hey, kid, get out of here," the ticket taker says when the woman in front of Willie shuffles off. "I already gave you your transfer."

Willie tries to explain, but the man cuts him off. "Look, kid, don't give me a hard time. I remember you, okay? I gave you a transfer. Now don't try to con me. Move along or I'll have to get someone to move you."

Disgruntled voices from behind float up. "Move it outta there, kid . . . We ain't got all day . . . Come on, mister, move him."

Willie shrugs and moves out of line and back toward the front exit. Okay. He'll just carry his bag and follow the instructions the guy gave him before. He won't look at anybody and he'll walk as fast as he can. Straight to the BART station. It can't be that dark on the street *all* the way there.

He's so rattled worrying about how to negotiate his way to where he's going, he doesn't realize that even without a transfer to the local bus, he could still ride for only sixty cents. Fear has thrown him off.

Strapping his duffel bag over his shoulder, he walks through the exit and heads into the darkness. Goose bumps run up his back and down his arms in waves as he passes desperate men standing against buildings, hears noises from blackened doorways. He looks directly at the ground, striking the concrete sidewalk purposely, in exaggerated fashion, with the metal tip of his cane. He tries to whistle, but his mouth is dry as dust. At the corner of the second block he stands, waiting for the

WALK sign, gripping the cane tightly, feeling the strap of his duffel bag absently with his bad hand.

"Boy," a voice says, and Willie starts, gripping the cane tighter. "You got fiffy cent?" It's a drunk; an old leathery man, hair greasy and gray, tattered sport coat pulled tight around his shoulders.

Willie stares at him as if he didn't hear.

"Jus' fiffy cent," the old man says. "Coffee. Buyin' me some coffee. Won' spen' it for booze. Gonna buy me some coffee."

Willie reaches into his pocket and comes out with all his change, dropping it into the man's cupped hands. The light changes and he walks away without a word, somehow feeling lucky all the guy wanted was a little money. He can't explain his fear, just knows it's there and it's real. The power and intensity of his mission fade again and he wishes he were back in Coho. He could stay away from Rhodes and Jenny, bury himself in his speech therapy; maybe even racquetball. He could live with Petey until his parents got things worked out. Maybe running away to the city was not all that great an idea; maybe he should just head back to the bus station and buy a ticket for home. Yeah. Crawl back after two days in the world; unable to make it, just like everyone is probably saying. No, not yet. A little longer.

In the dim streetlight at the end of the block, Willie sees a bus-stop sign and a bench. The sign has a BART logo and, according to the ticket man at the Greyhound terminal, that means at least some of the buses that stop there can take him to the subway. He's figured out his money is as good as a transfer and he can ride. At least the bus will be lighted. But people are at the bench, and they aren't just waiting for the bus. Kids. They look like kids, and as he approaches, he sees they're all Oriental, and young. One, a tall, thin boy probably not more than fourteen, stands on the edge of the bench, his leg kicking effortlessly out in front of him like a snake's tongue. The boy begins to turn slowly, kicking every forty-five degrees or so, his foot snapping in the air easily eighteen inches above his head. As his friends begin to cheer, he spins faster, flicking the foot effortlessly in all directions, lethally protected from all sides. Willie knows these guys are dangerous, even though they're young, but if he doesn't get on a bus pretty soon he'll be choked by his own heartbeat. He decides to wait at the bench; mind his own business and sit and wait. At the sound of his cane clicking on the concrete, the boy on the bench stops, turns simultaneously with his friends to silently greet Willie's approach. Willie nods and stands away from the bench, next to the bus-stop pole. The gang watches; Willie stares ahead. Finally the boy on the bench hops down lightly and approaches. "Hey, man. How you doin'?" Perfect English. Somehow Willie expected Chinese or something.

"Okay."

The boy nods, his friends filling in behind him. "Where you headed?"

". . . BART."

"What's that?"

Willie glances out of the corner of his eye, seeing the boy's face for the first time. He does look young; his face smooth as porcelain; cold eyes fixed on Willie's cane.

"A . . . cane."

The boy reaches out and takes it from Willie's grasp, holding the baseball head up to the light, reading: " 'Willie Weaver—1. Crazy Horse Electric—0.' You Willie Weaver?"

Willie nods. "My . . . friends. For . . . my leg."

"Crazy Horse. Ain't that an Indian?"

Willie nods again. That's all Crazy Horse is now. An Indian.

"What's the matter with your leg?" a voice from the small crowd behind. The kid who belongs to it can't be more than twelve, but he's as menacing as the rest. "You a crippled kid?"

Willie starts to answer, to explain, then just nods.

"You need this cane to walk?" the leader asks.

"Yes," Willie lies.

"You know we own this corner?"

Willie shakes his head. *Here it comes.*

"Well, we do. It costs you money to take the bus from here. You got money?"

Willie's so scared his knees actually feel as if they're going to just give way and leave him floundering on the sidewalk like a dying fish, but he concentrates hard, reaching casually for his cane. The boy moves it just out of reach. Willie says, "How . . . much?"

"How much you got?"

"Five. Maybe . . . six," he lies, regretting his money is all wrapped in a tight ball in his pocket. If he has to get it out, it'll all come at once; several hundred dollars. And if he gives up his money, he's done.

"Well, it costs six bucks to take the bus from here," the boy says. "You're a very lucky crippled kid."

"Maybe . . . I can . . . walk," Willie says, and reaches again for the cane.

"It costs six bucks to leave, too," the boy says evenly. "Or even to just stand here. We're businessmen. We have to make a living with our corner. It's the only one we own."

I'll bet, Willie thinks, but only grimaces, reaching into his pocket, hoping to be able to peel off a couple of bills

while making it appear that's all he has. *Please don't let
the whole roll come out.* As he slips the rubber band off
the roll inside his pocket, he hears a diesel engine roar
and glances up to see a bus rounding the corner, headed
for the stop. It pulls up to the stop and the doors open
with a hydraulic blast. The leader's attention is diverted
momentarily; Willie snatches the cane, stepping onto
the bus at the same moment. He reaches into his pocket
for the sixty-cent fare posted on the box. There is no
silver, only bills. He looks at the driver, who says, "Can't
make change." He peels a single off the roll, stuffing it
into the box, then looks up to see the gang leader watching over his shoulder.

"Six bucks, huh?" the boy says, leaning in close to
Willie's ear, and hands the driver a transfer. His buddies
board behind him.

Willie's heart sinks. He takes the seat directly behind
the driver and sits on the edge, his duffel bag between
his feet. The gang moves to the back of the bus. They're
laughing and joking; slapping each other around. And
they're stalking Willie Weaver.

"Could . . . you . . . tell me . . . when we . . .
get . . . to . . . BART?" he says to the driver, who
nods.

Willie sits staring out the front window, holding—
almost clutching—his duffel bag. He bends down to
look through the rear-view mirror back through the
bus, only to find the leader of the gang staring directly
back into his eyes. He leans back in the seat, closing his
eyes, fear—almost terror—welling up in his throat. *No
way out* telegraphs to him from the pit of his stomach.
He starts to cry; he doesn't want to because he knows
these guys can smell fear a mile away, but there's no

stopping it. Tears stream down his face as he wipes them furiously away.

"Those guys on your tail?" the driver asks. He's a big black guy with powerful arms hanging out of a short-sleeved uniform.

Willie's eyes pop open, startled. "Yeah," he says after a second. "I think so."

"Well, don' mess with 'em," the driver says. "Tha's a *bad* bunch. They want somethin', you give it to 'em."

Willie looks at his lap.

"Nothin' I can do, boy. What you doin' comin' outta neighborhood like that one anyway? After dark. Some kids got no sense."

Willie can only nod.

The driver sighs. "When we get to the station, I can maybe jam the back door a few seconds. You got to cross the street, so you get out the bus an' run like hell. Station's well lit. They got cops hang aroun' there some-times."

Willie looks up and smiles; resigned. "Thanks," he says. "I . . . can't . . . run . . . like hell. Used to. Can't . . . now."

"Well, I'll jam 'em as long as I can."

Willie reaches into his pocket and separates some of the money from the roll, pulls it out carefully, below the view line of the seat back, and runs it down the inside of his sock, under his arch inside the shoe. He hopes it's enough to get by on and he hopes he hasn't left the roll looking too small to fool the gang. He closes his eyes and waits for the BART station.

"It's comin' up, boy," the driver says. "Next stop. Get out and cross the street right in front of the bus. If it looks like trouble, I'll call the cops, but they won't get here quick; never do. You on you own."

The bus stops abruptly and Willie picks up his bag and steps slowly down off the step to the curb. The guys in the rear try to get out the back door, but the driver jams it. "Hey, bus driver, open the door!" the leader says. "Open the door, man. We want off here."

"I'm tryin'," the driver calls back. "Mus' be stuck. Come out the front."

Willie hears all that behind him as he tries to cross the street, but traffic is coming fast and he has to move down to the crosswalk. The light is red; he won't make it. He closes his eyes and waits. Maybe the driver will stall them a little longer; give him a chance to get to the lighted subway.

"You in a hurry?" The voice belongs to the gang leader.

". . . Kind of."

"Well, lemme take a look at what you got in your pocket there and you can go right on being in a hurry." His eyes are *so* cold; Willie is afraid to play games.

He reaches into his pocket and pulls out what is left of his roll of money, hands it to the kid, looking at his diminutive size, thinking *If I were okay, I'd beat this kid to death.*

"This isn't all. Don't be messing with the Jo Boys."

Willie holds his ground. "It's . . . all . . . I've got," he says.

"There was more."

"It's . . . all . . . I've got," Willie says again, evenly. ". . . Really."

The boy's foot flashes across the side of Willie's head so fast Willie doesn't even see it coming and he's kicked twice more before he hits the ground. His duffel bag skids away in one direction, his cane in another. Another of the gang members unzips the bag, emptying it onto the sidewalk; kicks the contents around, then searches the corners of the bag in case he missed the money. "Nothin' here, Kam," he says, and the leader, the boy called Kam, kicks Willie three more sharp blows to the ribs. Willie tucks, covering his face with his arms, praying it will be over soon.

Suddenly his face is pulled by the hair up to a spot inches from Kam's. "Give me the rest of the money, you crippled white turd, and I might let you stay alive." There's movement, a click and the flash of a blade.

"In . . . my . . . sock," Willie says through his bloody, already swollen lip. "Right . . . foot."

"Get it."

Willie sits up and the world swirls around him. He reaches for his shoe, but topples over as darkness crowds in from the sides. There's a loud thud and sharp pain shoots up the back of his neck, then his ribs begin to cave in. The back of his throat tastes of blood; Willie's sure he's being killed.

Somehow he kicks off his shoe, steps on the toe of his right sock with the heel of his left foot, and pulls the foot out of the sock. His money protrudes just above the neck of the sock and a gang member spots it. "Bingo!" he yells, and Kam stops the beating to look down, bending over easily to pick it up.

"Should have given us this in the first place," he says. "Don't mess with the Jo Boys."

Willie is balled up again, protecting his head, eyes closed, waiting.

"Got his cane, Kam," he hears. "Want it?"

"Naw. Leave 'im his cane. Might need it to walk." Kam's mouth is next to Willie's ear; a whisper. "Don't mess with the Jo Boys."

They're gone, but Willie doesn't move. He's paralyzed with fear and humiliation, and he doesn't know if he's okay; if anything's broken. Right now, right this minute, he'd give anything in the world to be back in Coho. Jenny could go out with anyone she wants; Mom and Dad could blame him for ruining their lives forever. He'd gladly take the blame and shut up. He never had any idea there was this in the world.

He tries to stand, gather his things, but the world swirls again and he drops to his knees. He grabs his cane, leaning against it with both hands on the ball, and struggles to his feet. One eye is swollen almost shut and he turns his head awkwardly to see his belongings scattered about the sidewalk. Bending down to gather them up, he pitches forward, striking his head against the side of the brick building next to the crosswalk, feeling the world slip away.

— CHAPTER 12 —

Willie awakens to find himself staring into the eyes of the bus driver. "Damn!" the driver says between clenched teeth. "Why you have to go ridin' *my* bus?"

Willie attempts to sit, but his head swirls and he eases it back to the concrete. He tries to speak; finds the effort too great. Slowly events crowd back into his head: Kam with his killer moves, Willie with his fear. He doesn't know why the bus driver's there or how long it's been; just hopes he won't leave again. He tries once again to sit up, this time successfully, and scoots back against the building while the bus driver silently picks up his belongings, carelessly stuffing them into the duffel bag. "You get up?" he asks gruffly.

". . . Yeah," Willie says, though he doesn't know it's true. He *will* get up, though, if it means this guy will help him off the street. "Why'd . . . you . . . come back?"

The driver shoots him a mean look. "Beats me," he says. "Got to be out of my mind. Damn cripple white boy got no better sense than be out here. You ain't from around here."

Willie shakes his head, feeling the swollen pressure of his eye and lip. "No. I . . . ain't . . . from . . . around here." His head clears some and begins throbbing with pain. He tries to push the pain out, but it floods over him and he drops to his knees, vomiting.

The driver stoops to hold Willie's shoulders, and his tenderness suddenly makes Willie furious. "Why . . . the hell . . . are you . . . helping me . . . now?" he screams between convulsions. "Where . . . were you . . . when . . . those guys . . . were . . . trying . . . to kill me?"

The driver makes no verbal response, but helps Willie to his feet. He hands Willie his cane, looking at the brass handle. "You Willie?"

Willie nods and snatches the cane with his good hand. He looks the driver in the eye, and his own eyes well up in tears. "Why . . . didn't you . . . help . . . me?" he asks quietly.

A look of shame sweeps across the driver's face like a flash flood, then disappears as quickly. He picks up Willie's bag. "Lacey my name," he says. "Get on the bus."

Willie isn't about to argue.

* * *

"I didn't help you 'cause you don't go takin' on a street gang," Lacey says across the table in Romano's. It's well after two in the morning. Willie rode the bus route for the past two hours, sleeping fitfully in the mostly deserted bus, waiting for Lacey's shift to end. "That wasn't jus' some buncha China boys out on a picnic. Tha's a street gang. They cut you or do you in for nothin'. Leave body parts scattered on the sidewalk for the kinda money you carryin'."

"*Was* . . . carryin'," Willie says.

"I *tol'* you to give 'em what they want," Lacey says. "Coulda save you young ass."

Willie lowers his eyes and nods. "I know," he says. "I . . . just . . . couldn't . . . afford . . . to lose . . . it . . . all."

"You done *los'* it. Got a face job in the deal."

Willie nods again, grimacing.

Lacey sits back and pushes away his empty plate. "So what I got to do to get you where you goin', 'sides pay up this bill?"

Willie shakes his head. ". . . Don't . . . know . . . where . . . I'm going," he says.

"You on the run?"

He nods again and suddenly pieces of the story tumble out, from his life back on the other side, to the Crazy Horse Electric game, to the accident, to Jenny, to his parents, to the decision to get on the bus.

"So here . . . I . . . am," he finishes.

"White boy gettin' three hot ones a day an' a warm bed coulda picked a lot better place to run to than Oakland, California," Lacey says, "even if he do be havin' hard times. You don't know what hard times *is* till you try makin' it on the street in this city."

Willie explains that he wasn't exactly coming to *Oakland*.

"May be," Lacey says. "But you here. An' this Oakland." He glances at the gold watch on his massive wrist. "Gettin' late," he says. "Got to decide what you wanna do. Be willin' to foot the bill to send you back, you wanna go. You got no binnis stayin'."

Willie takes a deep breath, exhaling slowly. "I . . . can't . . . go home," he says. "I . . . don't know . . . where, but . . . I can't . . . go home. Just . . . can't."

"Buncha pride ain't doin' you much good, boy. You got to make up you mind," Lacey says. "I don't got all night. You neither."

Willie takes a chance. "You . . . got . . . a place . . . I could . . . stay . . . till tomorrow . . . maybe?"

Lacey shakes his head quickly. "Can't be harboring no runaway," he says. "Don't need no extra attention from the police." He starts to elaborate, then shuts up.

"You . . . got a . . . family?"

Lacey shakes his head. "Got no family."

"One . . . night. I'd . . . sleep . . . on . . . the couch. No . . . trouble."

Lacey looks at Willie, shaking his head. "I know I shoulda lef' you. I come back, and jus' *know* you gonna cause me buncha trouble. 'Lacey,' I say in my head, 'Lacey Casteel, listen to me. What you gonna do you go back, find that boy down like you *know* you gonna? Makin' trouble you don't need like the dumb nigger you is.'" He looks at Willie long and hard again. "One night," he says. "Tomorrow you got to know what you doin'. One night. I help you with bread, but tha's it. Okay?"

"Okay," Willie says.

"Now don't be gettin' up tomorrow wantin' one more day," Lacey warns. "An' one more day after that."

Willie stands and reaches for his duffel bag, but Lacey picks it up ahead of him. He feels the residual pain in his ribs and muscles from the blows he's taken, and the cuts and bruises on his face seem to sting and ache more, but he's put at least twelve hours' insulation between himself and the world, and his mood picks up. This is survival.

He eases himself into the passenger's seat of Lacey's huge black Chrysler and sinks into the sheepskin seat, closing the one eye not already swollen shut, and tries to relax. Lacey lives away from the main part of town, toward the Oakland Hills, a fifteen-minute drive from the restaurant. Neither speaks as the Chrysler glides up Park Boulevard, turns left and winds its way through the lower-middle-class neighborhood—small and medium-sized houses standing so close to each other they look as if they're being packed to send somewhere—until it pulls into Lacey's driveway. Willie sits up to look around. The difference between the surroundings here and what he has just come from is immense. "Nice . . . place," he says.

"Don't go be gettin' used to it."

Inside, Lacey shows him only what's necessary: the bathroom, the fold-out couch, a corner to put his belongings in. Lacey's keeping a distance, but Willie senses the door isn't quite closed. He's been reading people since the accident and he has nothing to lose by being patient and maintaining a low profile. Something in this man feels for Willie, and Willie knows it. Maybe Lacey could actually get him started somewhere . . .

Willie wakes to the sun streaming through the window, directly into his eyes, on the pulled-out couch. His swollen eye is matted shut and every muscle feels as if he's been clubbed like a throw rug on a clothesline. The house is silent, and he pushes himself up to look out the window; the Chrysler is gone. He lies back, collecting his thoughts, trying to remember where the bathroom is. He'd give his good arm for a shower.

Drying off, he hears the rattling of paper sacks, the opening and closing of cupboards, and knows Lacey is back. He stays in the bathroom longer than necessary because he hasn't yet decided what to do and he's not ready to face Lacey pushing him to make a decision. He tries again to figure Lacey, who's telling him he has to go but the borders are a little fuzzy, like if maybe Willie plays it right Lacey might see clear to help him out with something more than just a bus ticket. Lacey's a tough guy. If he really just wanted Willie gone, he'd have no trouble making that happen. Willie's in no position to do anything but take what is given. He pulls on his jeans and T-shirt and walks slowly out into the living room.

"Decided what you gonna do?" Lacey calls from the kitchen.

"Not . . . for sure," Willie calls back. He's staring out the front window at Lacey's car, noticing for the first time the fancy pin-striping down the sides and the custom hood ornament. In the light of day it looks like every pimp's car on every show Willie has ever seen. "Not . . . going back . . . to Montana . . . though."

"Tha's smart," Lacey says sarcastically, standing in the kitchen door. "Maybe you wanna jus' find you a place down there close to the bus station. Keep you *apprised* what the world like."

Willie says he thinks he'll steer clear of the bus station for a while; maybe go back down there the day Hell freezes over.

"Won't be any safer then," Lacey says. "This jus' ain't a place for no Montana cowboy kid to run to. Don't you see that yet?"

"I can . . . see . . . that . . . with . . . one eye . . . swollen shut," Willie says, "but . . . I'm here." He glances up; Lacey looks real different than he did last night. He's decked out in a silk shirt open to the chest and skin-tight pants, with jewelry on almost every finger and a big gold chain around his neck. Willie looks back to the car.

"Got money for you ticket outta here right in my pocket," Lacey says. "Best offer you gonna get in this town."

"Know . . . about . . . any jobs?" Willie asks. ". . . Anything. Cleaning . . . buses. Fast . . . food."

"Bus jobs all union shit," Lacey says. "An' you got to have a work permit even at McDonald's."

"How about . . . I . . . work . . . for you?"

"Doin' *what?*"

Willie smiles and says he could work three days a week just keeping Lacey's car clean. He could fix up his house and yard; generally keep things up. It would only cost Lacey room and board, and as soon as something came up, Willie would move.

Lacey starts to say no, but stops. "Might add some class to my act if I got me a servant boy," he says. "Get you a little white jacket and a bow tie . . ."

Willie says he'll beg off on the jacket and bow tie, but he'll work real hard and stay out of the way. He can't believe it's this easy; that Lacey is actually considering it.

Lacey sits on the couch, seeming to think, then says, "I been thinkin' 'bout this; I know you was gonna ask. You know I ain't jus' a bus driver. Bus driver jus' be my cover. I deals in human relations. Management. You stay here, you got to keep you eyes an' ears an' mouth *shut*. Can you comprehend that?"

Management, Willie thinks. *Pretty funny. So he is a pimp.* But Willie's not about to get into a morals argument at this point. Something changed in him after last night, after he survived what he was sure was his last second on earth, and from now on Willie Weaver's going to take whatever he has to take to survive. "I . . . don't know . . . about . . . my eyes . . . and . . . ears," he says, "but . . . by . . . the time . . . I . . . ever . . . get . . . anything said . . . to anybody . . . they . . . forget . . . what I'm . . . talking about."

"One thing," Lacey says. "You stayin' 'cause of a reason you don't know, and I ain't gonna be explainin' it to you, so don't go askin'. Can you comprehend that? Also, you goin' to school. Don't wanna be wonerin' what you up to all day long. Got to keep outta my hair."

Willie will agree to anything, and he nods okay.

— CHAPTER 13 —

Lacey's car pulls up in front of the old school building and he flips the automatic gearshift into PARK. Willie stares out the tinted window at the building. A huge, colorful sign above the entrance announces the school's name: OMLC High School. The rest of the building, with its steep roofs and pillared overhangs, looks like a medieval mansion about to be pulled flat by gravity.

"What if . . . it . . . falls down . . . on . . . me?" he asks with a smile.

"Get under you desk or some shit," Lacey says back, without smiling. "Listen, this school don't look like much, but I know some kids come out here with some *tools,* Chief. So don't you go judgin' by the paint job. You go in there an' check it out." Lacey calls him Chief now because of the mention of Crazy Horse on Willie's cane.

"Only . . . foolin'," Willie says. He's learning when to give Lacey a hard time and when to stay clear of him. It's been a week now and Willie has worked hard for him. Lacey keeps his "management" business away from home, so there's been nothing to deal with there, and Willie spends most of his time cleaning and making minor repairs he learned to make working around his own house with Big Will in better days. He's smart enough not to get in Lacey's way; smart enough to know Lacey has a real mean streak and the best thing to do is stay as far away from it as possible. He still hasn't figured how Lacey came to let him stay and he doesn't know how long it will last; he doesn't ask.

It's the middle of the day and on the exterior the school appears deserted, but he walks through the entrance, hearing the familiar sounds of "business as usual." He's here for a pre-entry interview with the school's director, a guy named André Porter, who Lacey claims owes him many favors.

Willie hands André the required "résumé" he's been working on the past few days, detailing what he wants from OMLC and what he believes he has to offer it in return for admittance. André is a tall, rangy black man, built like a racehorse, with long, graceful hands and an easy, reassuring manner that immediately puts Willie at ease. There is no trace of Lacey's street dialect; this man sounds to Willie as if he were educated in Britain, though he has no English accent.

"You did a good job with this," he says, smiling, as he lays the paper on the table beside him.

Willie nods. "Thanks." He did do a good job, and was absolutely straight about the reasons he left home; crystal clear in his final statement that he was not going back to Montana; if he weren't accepted into OMLC, he would enroll in public school.

"Did Mr. Casteel tell you anything about our school?" André asks, leaning back in his swivel chair, fingers interlaced behind his head.

"Only . . . that . . . it's . . . a good one."

"Well, it's a good one, but it's a *different* one," André says. "Basically we're here for kids who aren't making it in the public schools, for whatever reason. That means we've got kids with learning disabilities, kids with attitude problems, kids with drug and alcohol problems, and kids whose parents just want them to have more attention than they can get in a class of thirty-five students where at least fifteen are armed and dangerous." He smiles. "You armed or dangerous?"

Willie puts his arms out, palms up, and looks down at himself with a self-effacing shrug.

"Guess not," André says. "Now, about tuition."

Willie looks up in embarrassed silence and swallows. He thought Lacey had worked this part out. *Damn it! Lacey knows he doesn't have any money.*

"My best guess would be," André goes on, "that Mr. Casteel told you I owe him big and my letting you in school here would be an infinitesimal beginning toward repayment. May have even told you he's my cousin."

"Something . . . like that." Willie guesses Lacey has referred other students here.

André shakes his head in amusement. "Mr. Casteel has what we in the educational community refer to as 'scrambled brains.' What I owe him is a long walk off a short pier, blindfolded, with his hands cuffed behind his back and a fifty-five-gallon drum filled with shot puts tied to his ankles."

Willie says it sounds like the two of them have different perspectives.

"That would be a way to put it," André says. "And if there were anything even remotely resembling Mr. Casteel in my family tree, I would personally have those branches sawed off and processed into Pres-to logs and toilet paper." André smiles. "You may have guessed by now that Lacey's a less-than-reputable member of this less-than-reputable community."

Willie allows that Lacey is not without his seamier side.

André laughs. "I like you, Willie. With that kind of diplomatic touch, you could be the first OMLC graduate to write copy for the White House. Anyway, Lacey Casteel's less-than-pristine reputation is none of your concern. Actually, I'm looking for some mellower folks to help balance things out around here, so you might be in luck. I've got two full work scholarships open right now. You interested?"

Willie nods, without any idea what that means.

"These work scholarships are a big deal," André says. "Every kid who goes to school here is either funded by a school district as a 'special needs' kid, or he pays tuition. We're private, nonprofit. That means almost no outside help, so we do our own janitorial work and what maintenance we can. That grassy playground area out there," he says, pointing out the window, "belongs to the city and is actually classified as a park; but we have an agree-

ment that we'll keep it up in return for use during
school hours. So there's lots of work to do."

Willie looks out over the flat area divided into sec-
tions of playground apparatus, open grassy areas with
benches and tables, a full basketball court and a large
patio next to the school. The park is in much better
repair than the school building itself.

"One thing you should know," André says, breaking
Willie's train of thought. "It's my intention to make this
place into something to be proud of, and we can't be
proud if it doesn't look good. We've got a lot of work to
do on the building—we've only been in here a year, and
this place was condemned—and before June of next
year I want it looking like a castle. So if you take this
scholarship, you'll have plenty of work to do. And if you
slough off on me, I can't afford to keep you, okay?"

Willie says that's okay with him. At this point he's still
concentrating on survival and this man is offering something significant.

"And you can tell Lacey Casteel I'm still as soft a
touch as ever." André laughs, then looks at Willie seriously. "I've got a feeling, though, that I might be getting
the better end of this deal."

"I . . . hope so," Willie says.

"So let me give you the tour."

The halls of OMLC are dimly lit, with mustard-
colored walls and high gray ceilings, but each classroom
is well lit from natural light streaming through large
windows and decorated in bright colors with posters
and charts and paraphernalia pertinent to the discipline
being taught there. Students look up curiously, sometimes suspiciously, as Willie and André stand briefly in
each doorway; teachers nod and smile, continuing their
lessons.

"You may be a little uneasy at first," André says, back in his office. "Some of these kids seem pretty damaged before you get to know them. Some of them seem pretty damaged *after* you get to know them, but I'm sure there are friends for you here, and you can get a good education if you want it."

Willie's feeling a little confused about what to do. He could go to public school for nothing—not have to work. This place obviously operates on a shoestring; he didn't see one piece of audiovisual equipment, not even a film projector. There are desks and teachers and books.

For no concrete reason, he trusts André. "Would . . . you go . . . here . . . or . . . to regular . . . school . . . if . . . you were . . . me?"

André looks at him; takes him in from top to bottom, honestly considering. "Your résumé says you're pretty smart but have a hard time showing it because of your 'handicap,' " he says. "Inner-city schools don't always have the resources to figure that out. We don't have a class here with more than twelve kids in it, and at least a third of our teachers have degrees to work with special-needs kids. You won't get that in public school." André looks at Willie more seriously. "If you go into a public school, you'll have to change your act. The way you're looking right now has 'victim' written all over it, and you'd be in the Oakland High district. Takes an act of Congress to go out of district, so you'd be pretty much stuck with O-Hi." He thinks a second, then says firmly, "I'd go here."

Willie shrugs. "Here it is." He's curious. "Why . . . OMLC? I mean . . . why . . . do they . . . call it . . . that?"

"Named after our fictitious founding fathers," André says. "Owens, McMurray, Lincoln and Caldecott."

"They're . . . fictitious?"

"Yeah. Never heard of any of them. Except Caldecott. He has a tunnel named after him. What it really stands for is One More Last Chance." He laughs. "When we started this place, I kept kicking kids out, then letting them back in, when they begged and pleaded, for one more last shot at it. When we rented the building down by Lake Merritt, we called it Lakeside, which I think was awfully clever, don't you? The lady I was married to worked with me then. She named it. She had the imagination of an artichoke, but that's another story. Anyway, when we moved up here, I wanted to give us a name that meant something, so I did. Board thought it was a great idea."

With a loud crack, the door flies open; a tall, gangly blond kid slides around the door jamb and turns to face André, his back to Willie. His collar is buttoned right up to the top; his shirt tail half in, half out. The metal tip of his too-large cowboy belt whacks against the door jamb as he turns. He wears a full set of telephone repair tools on his hip, giving him the appearance of an AT&T gunslinger from outer space. "This school is a chickenshit rip-off!" he booms in a deep bass voice that belies everything about his appearance.

André's head jerks up, surprised, but he regains his composure almost instantly. "Hi, Jack," he says. "This is Willie Weaver. He's looking around to see if he wants to go to school here."

Jack turns his head to Willie, seeming startled to realize there's someone else in the room, then snaps his head back around to face André. "This school is a chickenshit rip-off," he says again.

"You're here to tell me something more specific than that," André says.

Jack stops to think, looking a little stunned. "This school is a chickenshit rip-off," he says once more, his voice even deeper. *This guy could be an opera singer,* Willie thinks absently, and sits waiting to find out why the school is a chickenshit rip-off.

"You don't pay any money to go here, Jack," Andre says. "How is it we're ripping you off?"

"You said it was safe."

"Somebody teasing you again?"

Jack gives a big nod in the affirmative. "Joel. He's a butt. He's a dirty butt. He's a filthy, slimy butt." Jack begins to delight himself with the possibilities, forgetting for a moment why he stormed in. "Joel is a filthy, putrid, slimy—"

"That's enough," André breaks in. "We get the point. What did he do?"

"My nose."

André nods. "He said it was too big?"

Jack nods back. "He's a filthy, stinking—"

"Hey, Jack," André says, "give me a break. Joel's a butt, okay?"

"Yeah," Jack says, "a stinking, putrid, filthy—"

André has worked his way over to Jack and simply clamps his hand over Jack's mouth. "Your mom let you talk like that at home?" he asks.

Jack stops, seemingly stunned again. "You gonna tell her?"

"Do I need to?"

Jack's head shaking "no" is more like a vibration than a recognizable gesture.

"All right, then," André says. "Lighten up. What did we decide we were going to do the next time Joel said your nose was too big?"

Willie involuntarily pictures the scene in Mr. Small's office if some kid from Coho High stormed into the principal's office loudly declaring the value of the school in the currency of chicken waste. He shudders. This experience at OMLC will be different.

Jack's lost expression says he doesn't remember.

"What does Joel want when he does that?" André asks.

"To make me mad."

"Right. And when it works, when you get mad, who wins?"

"That filthy, putrid—"

"Joel. Right. If he doesn't make you mad, who wins?"

"Me."

"Right again," André says. "Who do you want to win?"

"Me," Jack answers definitely.

"So what do you have to do?"

Jack smiles. "Whistle Dixie. Walk off. Mark up a win." Obviously André's terms.

"Okay," André says, sitting back in his chair. "Get back out there and win one for the bitcher."

Jack is charged. He performs something close to an about-face and marches out the door. André lets out a big sigh and shakes his head, smiling over at Willie. "Tunnel vision," he says. "Jack can't focus on *anything* when something's bothering him. He's a whiz with telephones, though. Only kid I ever met who actually wants to grow up to be a telephone repairman."

Willie smiles, looking out the empty doorway.

"Don't judge the place by Jack," André says, reading Willie's mind. "We only have a couple of those real exotic flowers. And it kind of adds a flavor to the place."

* * *

Near midnight, Willie lies in his makeshift bed at Lacey's place counting the rainbow dots on the wall and ceiling created by the streetlight shining through raindrops on the window, aching for Jenny, and Coho; his real life. The urge is overwhelming to call her on the phone, or at least to call Johnny, and tell them where he is; that he's all right and doesn't want them to worry; to leave a message for his mom and dad saying he loves them; something. He knows he can't—won't. Not yet, at least. He wonders if Jenny will ever realize that telling him the truth was way more important to him than whether or not she went for someone else; he'd been *so* tired of having to read people rather than having them come out and say what was on their minds; and that's the one place he needed her to be different. He wonders, too, if the poor kid in the Portland bus terminal ever mailed his postcards from Phoenix.

And suddenly there's Missy, his baby sister who never did anything with her life but suck her fingers and make funny noises and drool. He sees her lying there in the crib, smiling around her fist, looking right into his soul. There was such a clear, wonderful connection there. Willie would protect her as she grew; shield her from the tough times. They both knew that. Then, as instantly and irretrievably as the tip of a water ski cracking into a promising young athlete's head, Sudden Infant Death Syndrome. Willie was embarrassed back then to tell his parents how he sometimes sat in her room looking down at her, his index finger tightly clutched in her tiny hand, planning for her life. And now he's just another death in the family.

— CHAPTER 14 —

"So find your center," Lisa says, and Willie watches the kids lined up in rows in front of her close their eyes and feel for a spot somewhere just above the navel. What he doesn't notice is that the spot is different on each person. "Now picture yourself playing whatever game you're choosing today," she says, pausing to give them time to form it behind their closed eyes, "and see yourself making every move from your center. Your center moves first, then the rest of your body follows. Your arms and legs don't get away from you that way. You play under control."

Willie isn't enrolled in this class, which is all-school PE. He has an agreement with André to stay out of PE until he's ready, or for three weeks, whichever comes first; so this is a study time for him. He's decided that if he has to be in PE eventually, he'd better come out and look; see what he might be able to salvage out of it. PE holds the threat of extreme embarrassment.

"Okay," Lisa is saying. "Basketballers on the court, soccer on the west, Ultimate Frisbee on the east. Those of you who said you want to run have a course laid out." She smiles. "I believe, children, that I have found a way, with the help of neighbors and local merchants, to make sure you run the whole course. I want each of you to take one of these three-by-five cards with you when you go. When you come back, I want the initials of Mr. or Mrs. Jameson—that's the elderly couple at 1014 Sinto; one of them will be on the porch—somebody at the doughnut shop next to the mall, and somebody at the Michelin Tire store on Broadway and Cedar. They all know the deal. If you don't have the initials, you don't get credit for the day. I refuse to give you high-school credit for walking over to the park to smoke dope."

There are a few protests, but they die quickly; Lisa 'has been around long enough that no one expects to change her mind.

Some of the kids wear shorts, or *some* form of gym gear; others remain in street clothes, but the one requirement is that everyone participates in *something*. The soccer field has no side boundaries and there seems to be no limit to the number of players on a side, so within minutes the game takes on a chaotic structure focused only on getting the ball from one end of the park to the other and between the two fluorescent cones—obtained from the California Highway Department at drastically reduced prices—which represent goals. The only obstacles more treacherous to the ball handler than the defensive players are the players on his or her own team, each of whom has an almost manic inner drive to score. Pelé would not recognize this game.

Ultimate Frisbee, a kind of cooperative volleyball game played with a plastic disk, is quieter but structured much the same. No matter how carefully he watches, Willie still can't discern what measures success. The basketball game is more recognizable: full court, no referee but with offensive players calling the fouls. It's run-and-gun street ball, and some of the players are really talented athletes, though Willie sees none of the discipline he's used to from his years and years in organized sports. Lisa, stripped down to T-shirt and shorts, plays point guard on one of the teams. She's kicking butt. Most of the players on the court are faster and most can certainly jump higher, but Lisa never tries anything she doesn't already know she can do. If the shot isn't there, she passes. She gets all the garbage rebounds: any- and everything that comes off the rim funny; a sixth sense tells her where it will be. She knows where the ball is all the time and she knows where everyone else on the court is. Willie recognizes something in her play that reminds him of himself when he played sports; it's the thing that made him better than all the others, gave him a constant edge. He watches the game, anticipating Lisa's moves, and more often than not he's right. He can almost feel himself moving with her.

"Play?" a voice behind him booms. Willie turns to see Jack, basketball under his arm, dressed in white gym trunks and a gray sweatshirt with PETERBILT carefully lettered in Magic Marker across the front. His telephone equipment hangs on his hip and he wears street shoes with black dress socks.

Willie smiles. "No . . . thanks. I'm . . . just gonna . . . watch."

"Can't," Jack booms. "Got to play. You'll get an 'F.' "

Willie starts to explain that he's not in the PE class yet, that he's just checking it out.

"Can't check it out," Jack says. "You got to play something or they give you an 'F.' "

Willie tries another tactic. "We . . . can't play . . . here," he says. "They've . . . got . . . the court."

Jack turns and points to a basket mounted on a wooden backboard up against the school. It's lower than regulation by at least a foot and tilts down on the right side at least three inches. It looks like a basket designed to fit Willie's new body structure and it's far enough away from where most people are playing that no one would notice. He decides why not.

"Make it, take it," Jack says. "By ones to eleven." He's been listening to the big boys play. "Do or die." He launches a shot from the top of the faded key; a high rainbow that whips through the net without even touching the rim. "My outs," he says and begins to bounce the ball with both hands.

Willie hasn't touched a basketball since way before his accident and has no idea whether he can even shoot anymore; or dribble.

Jack's second shot bounces off the rim and he doesn't even attempt to rebound it as it bounces into Willie's hands. Willie takes it, trying to establish some kind of rhythm, dribbling with his right hand and dragging his left side along. Jack doesn't play much defense, except to jump up and down in front of him yelling, "Hey, man!" so it's pretty much Willie against himself. He finally does get a primitive kind of rhythm and moves in close on the right side of the basket, flipping the ball underhanded toward the hoop. It bounces off the rim and Jack snatches it up, yelling, "Showtime!" as he two-hands it out to the top of the key. He turns, plants his feet wide and shoves another rainbow high into the air, screaming, "Two!" as the ball whips again through the bottom of the net.

Jack sinks two more from the same spot before Willie gets the ball back and works it slowly, methodically, in for a point of his own. By now the main basketball game has broken up and players are moving over to see what exotic athletic contest is taking place on Jack's court, and Jack is building up a cheering section.

This is Willie's worst nightmare: a crowd of strangers standing around watching what he has become. He holds it together, though; pats Jack on the back and says, "Good game, Jack. I gotta go finish a paper."

"Eleven!" Jack yells. "We go to eleven! You can't quit. That would be a chickenshit rip-off!"

Someone in the growing crowd yells, "Come on, finish the game!" and Jack gives a big nod. "The fans want it," he says.

Willie's claustrophobic. There's no way out except to play, and now Jack is getting excited, running a weird commentary on the play, bringing way more attention to them than would normally accompany the nightmare. Embarrassment edges toward humiliation, but Willie brings the ball in, protects it with his bad side and works toward the hoop. Jack makes a few halfhearted attempts at slapping it away, but he's more interested in his running commentary: "Gimp protects the ball and moves in. Telephone Man is playing him like a blanket. *Like a blanket.* It's a matter of time before he'll snatch the ball from the greedy clutches of Gimp and sink it big time. Gimp doesn't have a chance, folks. He's a white guy. White guys can't play this game. Telephone Man is all colors. He's a rainbow. And he can sky."

The banter from the crowd, which includes almost everyone now, is good-natured, directed at egging Jack on rather than humiliating Willie, and Willie is making himself invisible, smiling as Jack talks and letting him take his shot.

The crowd parts at the side of the court to let Lisa through, and she walks onto the court. "Willie," she says, walking close, "do you want to finish this?"

He starts to say "No," but hears the crowd yelling to let it continue; to "let Telephone Man show his stuff." He shrugs instead. "It's okay," he says. "No harm."

Lisa looks into his eyes, sees that anything would be

better than this attention, and turns to Jack, moving real close to his ear. "His name is Willie," she says evenly. "You have some respect. You call him that."

In his best Pavarotti voice, Jack says, "Yes, ma'am." He turns to Willie. "Didn't mean to call you that."

Willie just nods. Jack brings the ball in, dribbling with both hands, deliberately moving to his spot. "Telephone Man, you one *sweet* ball-handler," comes from the crowd. "Man can *bounce* that ball." Then, "He nose dribble better than he do," and Jack comes on point, whirling to face that voice, his telephone equipment perpendicular to his body like a ballerina's tutu as he spins. "There's nothing wrong with my nose!" he booms. His face looks like a road map of Mars as the blood rushes in, and his entire body stiffens. "There's nothing wrong with my nose, Joel! I heard you! I know you're there!"

Willie, seeing Jack's about to go up in smoke, limps over to him. "Let's . . . just . . . play," he says quietly. "There's . . . nothing wrong . . . with . . . your nose."

"They just won't leave me alone!" Jack yells and his voice starts to go high. "They won't leave me alone!" He's squealing now, falling into a heap. Willie tries to hold him up, but he isn't ready and Jack is heavy. They both topple. Behind them in the crowd, Willie hears someone chastising Joel for his remark, but Joel says something about the kid's mother and the crowd begins to break. Secretly, though Willie feels bad for Jack, he's glad someone did something—anything—to break up the game. At the rate he was scoring, it could have gone on forever, and he felt more and more naked as it continued.

"Willie, could I see you in the office for a minute?" It's Lisa.

"Sure. Just . . . a . . . sec."

"Whenever you're ready."

Willie walks into the office as Lisa kicks André out. "I need to talk to Willie," she says. "Alone. Why don't you go out back and flush out some dope fiends, or something else useful?"

André slaps her on the butt on his way out and she whirls around in mock anger. "In your wildest dreams," she says and leads Willie on in.

Lisa sits in André's chair and motions for Willie to sit in the chair next to the desk. "Pretty embarrassing out there, I guess," she says.

Willie nods. "I . . . guess . . . so."

"I thought you weren't going to join PE yet."

He shrugs. "Just . . . watching. Jack . . ."

Lisa nods, thinking. "You protect the ball. Ball-handling's not bad, all things considered. You've played before."

"Yeah. A . . . long time . . . ago."

"How old are you?"

"Almost . . . seventeen."

"Couldn't have been too long ago, then."

"Seems . . . like it," Willie says.

Lisa stands up thoughtfully and walks around the desk, sits on the corner and pulls a knee up under her chin. "Your condition is new, right?"

Willie looks puzzled.

"You weren't born like this."

Willie smiles and looks down. "No. I . . . wasn't . . . born like . . . this."

"How long ago?" Lisa asks.

"Less . . . than . . . a year."

"Have you had any therapy?"

"I had . . . this . . . counselor . . ."

"No, I mean physical therapy. Has anybody worked with you on physical rehabilitation?"

"I . . . did some . . . exercises," Willie says. "And . . . I run . . . some."

Lisa nods. "Yeah. That's not what I mean. Look, I'm studying for a Master's in Recreational Therapy and I've studied a lot of physical therapy, too. Actually, sports medicine. Would you be willing to try some things with me? Rehab things?"

Willie shrugs. "Sure. But . . . I . . . can't . . . pay . . . or anything."

Lisa laughs. "No," she says. "This will be as much for me as you. You get the benefit, I get a paper. Like a partnership."

Willie says that sounds good and starts to get up to leave, but Lisa stops him. "Stand there a second," she says and walks over. "Do you know where your center is?"

Willie remembers watching the kids at the beginning of PE. He points just above his navel. "Here . . . I . . . guess."

Lisa puts her hands on his shoulders to square them, then stands back. "Probably not," she says. "That probably was your center at one time, but—" she looks closer, squinting—"not now. Close your eyes."

Willie obeys.

"Now stand there and relax," she says, and Willie's left shoulder slides down a little, pushing the rest of his left side down with it. "Okay," Lisa says, "now let all the tension drain out through your feet; the only muscles you're using are those you need to stand there."

Willie relaxes more.

"Let it drain," she says. "All the tension is liquid and it's running out the bottoms of your feet."

Willie pictures a thick, dark liquid moving through his body toward gravity; his body relaxes more.

"Now put both arms out in front of you, with your fingers touching." Willie does as he's told. "And bring them back to what feels like the center of your body. Not what *looks* like the center; what *feels* like the center."

Willie's fingertips go directly to the place.

"Now open your eyes and look at it," Lisa says, and Willie looks down to the spot—which is significantly to the right of his navel and a little higher than he would have expected.

"That's the spot," Lisa says. "What you want to do now is, any time you're doing something physical, especially athletic, move your entire body from that place. In other words, move that place first and let your body follow." She gets up and slaps him on the butt. "That'll help."

Willie watches her walk out the door, his fingertips still touching his "center" lightly. He pokes himself hard there so he'll remember where it is. He doesn't really understand this at all, but he watched her play ball against guys with a hell of a lot more physical weaponry than she had, and hold her own. He picks up his cane, twirling it in his right hand, and moves out of the office, center first.

— CHAPTER 15 —

Music blares from the tape in Lacey's stereo system as Willie shuffles across the hardwood floor in the dining room. He's moving to the beat "from his center" the way Lisa's been showing him for the past three weeks, and it's beginning to feel more comfortable. "Just incorporate what you've got into your act," she said after their first session, and Willie is learning that when the music's too fast, you can cut the beat in half and be cool.

During the second session, Lisa showed him miles and miles of films and tapes over at the Alameda County Coliseum; sequences of famous athletes moving slow. One tape was nothing but a series of Jim Brown, the legendary running back for the Cleveland Browns back in the fifties and sixties, getting up from one after another vicious collision with some giant, faceless defensive lineman or linebacker. "See," Lisa said, "you can never tell if he's hurt or not. He always gets up and moves back to the huddle like he's taking his last step. It's part of his act. Could be he's lost all the feeling from his neck down and could be he's just taking his time." Then she showed him similar sequences of O. J. Simpson and Marcus Allen. "It's all slow, but look how graceful. You can move like that, too, Willie, if you'll quit trying to make your slow side catch up all the time. Do it the other way around. Try it to music."

So Willie is trying it to music. He knows if Lacey catches him playing this "honky rock-and-roll shit" on his sound system, he'll crap his drawers, but Willie sees so little of Lacey these days he's not really worried about it. Lacey is usually in bed in the morning when Willie leaves for school, and it's extremely seldom he sees him afterward because Lacey's either on his bus route or on the street. And most of the time when he is home, the time is taken up with these vicious telephone calls from his ex-wife, after which Lacey finds at least a dozen different ways to call her a bitch, storming around the kitchen kicking walls and slamming his fist against cupboard doors. It seems more than mere anger to Willie; more like agony. He doesn't know what it's all about—Lacey's been *real* clear it's none of his business —but he's told himself a million times he does *not* want to be there the day the two of them come face to face. Several days ago, Willie talked to André a little about it, while they were painting the student lounge, and André said if it got too bad, Willie could move into the empty classroom in the basement of the school; André had plenty of furniture at home, and the added security of having someone inside the school twenty-four hours a day wouldn't be all that bad an idea. Willie considered it, but decided against it for now because, even though they spent so little time together, he felt that Lacey was attached to him somehow; that it would be a small betrayal to leave.

Bob Seger starts into the even beat of "Fire Lake" on the sound system and Willie tries a slow heel-toe, heel-toe across the hardwood floor, looking down at himself and laughing self-consciously when he realizes if he keeps it up another few seconds his right side will run away from his left side and he'll be doing splits on the floor. Heel-toe will have to wait. It's after ten and he decides he better get with his homework, moving to the stereo to stop the record just as Lacey storms through the door. He's talking loud, though not angrily, and

Willie knows he's drunk. The swinging door from the kitchen flies open and Lacey yells, "Chief! How you doin', my man?"

Willie starts to answer, then sees Lacey's not alone. He's followed by a young girl; a girl Willie knows from school. She's tall and willowy, really beautiful to Willie, with light brown skin and green eyes. Willie has always seen her as quiet; either arrogant or really shy; and soft. But tonight she looks different, her painted lips and heavy rouge masking the softness and her plunging neckline immediately sinking Willie's heart. She works for Lacey.

"This Angel," Lacey says. "She go to you school. Get her some *outstanding* grades. Get some outstanding grades for *me,* too."

Willie tries to hide his disappointment. ". . . Hi," he says. "I'm Willie."

"I know," she says. "I see you sometimes."

"You . . . know Lacey, huh?" Willie says, and Angel's eyes go to the floor.

She nods, but before she can speak, Lacey says, "We have a *workin'* arrangement. An *outstanding* workin' arrangement." He looks to the sound system. "You playin' that honky shit on my *machine?* Them voices is in-*fer*-ior; mess up my speakers. Be gettin' them white boys *off* there."

Willie starts toward the system again, but the record is finished, the arm moving to its rest. He shrugs. "Over," he says. Then, "Well, listen . . . Got . . . to go. Get . . . some sleep." His speech is getting better; lots better, thanks to Lisa. She's getting him to work on that the same way he does his body; see things first—or hear them in the case of his speech—then go about them at a speed that works. He's not as embarrassed to talk now. "You guys . . . have a good . . . time."

Somewhere late in the night Willie hears a scream in the house and in a flash sits up in his makeshift bed. Chills run up his back as he waits, sure he heard it, but tempted by the possibility it was a dream. He hears it again, followed by Lacey's voice: mean. Willie throws back the blankets, moves quickly across the living room toward the stairs, scraping his shin on the coffee table lost in the dark. He hears the scream again and a loud bump, as if someone has been thrown down. He flips on the light and grabs his cane, starting up the stairs, calling Lacey's name.

At the bedroom door he stops, hoping that it's over; that he can just go down to bed; but there's more scuffling and Angel screams again. The sound of Lacey's open hand on her soft flesh sickens Willie and he hits the door with his cane. "Hey, Lacey. What's . . . going on . . . in there?"

No answer. Just more yelling.

"Lacey! Come on . . . you guys! What's . . . going on?"

"Git away!" Lacey yells from inside. "This none you damn binnis!"

"Come on!" Willie yells back. "Someone's . . . gonna get hurt!"

"Be you, you don' get back from that door!"

Another scream and the sound of scurrying. The door opens and Willie sees Angel's face briefly as Lacey pulls her back into the room and punches her in the jaw with his closed fist.

"Stop it!" Willie screams at him, but Lacey is cocking his arm for another shot. He pulls Angel's head up by the hair with his other hand and aims a fist for her nose. Without thinking, Willie swings the cane, intercepting Lacey's swing at the wrist, and now Lacey screams, dropping to his knees and clutching his arm. Willie comes back with the cane as hard as he can and the brass baseball catches Lacey in the back of the neck, whipping his head back hard, then driving his face into the floor.

Angel is stunned. She's uncovered from the waist up, kneeling by the bed, staring at Willie. "Oh, God," she says. "Why did you do that? When Lacey wakes up, he'll kill you."

Willie is trembling. He acted out of instinct, and now fear washes over him. Lacey *will* kill him if he wakes up. He stands over Lacey, swearing that if he moves, he'll club him again. He can't think; looks back to Angel. "Cover . . . yourself up," he says, and she reaches up to pull the bedsheet over herself. "Go downstairs . . . and . . . call Emergency. We'll . . . get him . . . to a doctor. That'll . . . give him . . . time to cool off."

Angel is still stunned; her nose is bleeding and the side of her face is starting to swell, but she moves around the bed, pulls on her blouse and picks up the phone.

Lacey hasn't regained consciousness when the ambulance arrives, and they put him in on a stretcher. Angel stays out of sight because she fears the police will show once the paramedics see the nature of the injuries, and she wants no part of that. Willie tells them Lacey got real drunk and pitched down the stairs, and though they seem skeptical, they hurry him off. Willie says he'll follow in Lacey's car, but he has no intention of doing so. He's going to pack his stuff. The medics assure him Lacey will stay the night in the hospital even if he regains consciousness. That gives Willie until tomorrow to pack and be gone. He absently gets the name and number of the hospital.

"Might as well . . . stay," he says to Angel as soon as the ambulance has carted Lacey off. "He won't be coming back here tonight."

Angel shakes her head. "You're in trouble, Willie. We're both in trouble. When Lacey gets back, he'll kill us both. You shouldn't have done that."

Willie doesn't get it. She should be grateful; Lacey was beating hell out of her. He can only stare.

"Christ," she says, "I've been beat before. I get over it. But he's gonna be killing mad."

Willie nods. There's a lot he'll never understand. He's known about Lacey's mean streak all along, but he's steered clear of it; never seen it so frighteningly close. He doesn't know how to handle it.

"If . . . he stays . . . in the hospital," Willie says, "I'll go . . . talk to him; make sure . . . he knows . . . it wasn't your fault."

Angel just laughs. "You don't get it, do you? Lacey's a *pimp.* He doesn't care whose fault it was. He just gets even. A pimp has to be mean or he won't make a living."

Fear creeps in. Willie knows Angel is right. But he's tired of being scared and he's tired of doing what he thinks is right only to have it turn out wrong. "Well, he . . . won't be back tonight, so you . . . might . . . as well get . . . some sleep."

Willie lies under the blankets on the couch, trying to get some sleep himself, but his mind races. Angel is upstairs, supposedly asleep, and he hates it that he can't feel like a hero. Even if she does work for Lacey, he's still very much drawn to her; emotionally—sexually—

drawn. He *should* be able to feel like a hero with her, but the rules are different here; all she can think of is how nasty Lacey's going to be. Tomorrow he'll move into the basement room at the school. To hell with Lacey. His mind glides over conversations with Angel: future conversations, convincing her to quit working for him. Maybe André can help.

Early in the morning Willie packs his stuff into his duffel bag, makes up his bed, throwing his sheets into the hamper in the laundry room. He leaves the duffel bag next to the door, stuffs his books into his backpack and walks through the overcast morning to the bus stop. Earlier he knocked on the bedroom door to check on Angel, but she had gone. He plans to ride up to school and cover his a.m. janitorial work, then ask André to let him skip morning classes to go check on Lacey. Dealing with him in the hospital will be a lot easier than facing him at home.

André just shakes his head when Willie tells him the story. "You can set up the room downstairs after school. I'll get a bed in there tonight, and we can move the furniture this weekend. I figured sooner or later your living situation would blow. Actually, it lasted longer than I expected."

Willie asks if André had known about Angel.

"Yeah," André says. "She's the reason I even know Lacey. Enrolled her two years ago. Said she was his daughter." He shakes his head. "I've seen enough shit go down since then to know that young lady is *not* Lacey Casteel's daughter."

"Why didn't you . . . stop her?"

"Ain't my job." André mimics one of Lacey's favorite sayings. Then, "Those aren't the choices I get to make for kids here. I can only offer an education and what advice is asked for. After you've been around awhile, you'll figure out that getting out of prostitution isn't just a question of deciding to stop one day. There's a *lot* more to it than that."

Willie parks André's '69 VW bug in the hospital parking lot, lifts his cane from the backseat and walks easily around toward the front entrance, moving slowly, from the center. The change in his movement has been just short of miraculous for him, and the good feeling it gives him is reminder enough to keep him focused. It's seldom now that his body gets away from him.

As he nears the information desk, his heart pumps almost out of control and he fights for some kind of inner calm, acquiring Lacey's room number from the nurse, then moving down the hall toward the elevator, silently rehearsing what he'll say. His mental words are drowned out by the drumbeat of his heart. In front of room 306 he takes a deep breath and steps through the open door.

Lacey lies sleeping, his right arm in a cast to the elbow, his neck in a brace. Willie can't believe *he* did that. He stands over Lacey for a moment, then places a hand on his muscular upper arm. Lacey's eyes pop open. He focuses on Willie's face, struggling to place him, then squints his eyes and gives a grimace.

"How . . . you doing?" Willie asks, for lack of a better start.

"Be okay. Can't say the same for you, though. Not when I get outta here."

"C'mon, man. I . . . thought you . . . were going to . . . kill her."

"She my whore."

"I . . . know that. But I thought . . . you . . . were going to kill her."

"She my whore," Lacey says again.

Willie doesn't pursue it. "Look," he says. "I'm . . . sorry I had to . . . hit you. If . . . you get even . . . you get even. I'll . . . be gone . . . when you get out of here. I'm going . . . to stay at the school. I . . . really appreciate all . . . you've done. I don't know how . . . I would have made it if you hadn't . . . taken me in. But I can't be around . . . what happened last night. I just can't. If . . . there's a way . . . I can make it up, let me know."

Lacey doesn't respond. Willie's surprised he doesn't make more threats, but he just stares. Willie thinks it must be whatever drugs they have him on. "By the way," he says, "your ex-wife, or . . . whoever she is, called. She . . . sounded pretty pissed. Says . . . she'll call later." He pauses a moment before saying, "She called you a killer."

A fire lights behind Lacey's eyes momentarily; is extinguished by welling tears. Willie sees a beaten look he hasn't seen ever before in Lacey. He doesn't understand. He says, "Look, I . . . gotta go . . ."

Lacey nods, but as Willie reaches the door, he says, "Don' move out yet, okay?"

"What?"

"I won' kick you ass. We talk. Jus' don' move out yet."

"Yeah, okay. Sure. You . . . sure?"

"Yeah, I'm sure." Lacey sounds irritated. He doesn't like to ask for things.

This is turning out differently than Willie expected. He sees no threat, so he just nods and leaves.

* * *

School is out and Willie leans against the rest-room wall, pulling on his basketball shoes. He's finished with his janitorial duties and Lisa is supposed to come back to work with him. He's wishing he could contact Angel, tell her he thinks everything's all right. She wasn't at school today; he didn't expect her to be, but he hopes she hasn't disappeared or something. André gave him a phone number from the files, but no one answers. He walks out toward the lawn as Lisa pulls her car close against the fence. When she steps out, he sees she's carrying leg and ankle weights; a basketball under her arm.

"Need to get an idea what it feels like to be you," she says, strapping on the weights.

"It feels . . . shitty to be me."

"I mean I need to know what your body feels like."

"You might need . . . more weights," Willie laughs. "Feels . . . more like a hundred pounds . . . than five."

"I have more if I need them."

A group of neighborhood kids stops their half-court game as Willie and Lisa start down at the other end. Everyone knows Lisa, and Willie feels embarrassment creeping up as it always does when he tries something in front of people. He fights it back and the kids resume their game.

Willie and Lisa shoot around awhile. At one point she stops and carefully watches him dribble and shoot lay-ups, then runs back to her car and adds five pounds onto her leg. She works with his shot; gets him to picture how he used to do it, then adjust that to what he can do now. It's frustrating, but after a half-hour or so, Willie starts to feel something familiar, and he works harder. After another fifteen minutes, they play a slow version of one-on-one. Lisa stops occasionally to help him make an adjustment, and occasionally to visualize an adjustment of her own because of the weights, so the game is interrupted, but when they're finished, Willie's worked up a sweat and it's the first time since the accident he's done anything positive with his body.

"Think you could beat Telephone Man today?" she teases.

Willie smiles. "Nope. He . . . can sky."

"In his *head* he can sky." She shakes her head and smiles. "Telephone Man. Whew."

Willie stops, philosophical for a moment. "I just wish I knew why."

"Why *what?*"

"Why me."

"You mean why you got hurt? Why you crippled yourself?"

Willie grimaces and nods. Lisa always words things like that; *why you crippled yourself* instead of *why you got crippled,* which he prefers.

She sits in the doorway of her car, pulling off her shoes. "What would be different if you knew why, Willie? You'd still be crippled."

"I know, but . . . if there's a reason; a *purpose.*"

"I'm going to do you a favor. I'm going to tell you why."

Willie waits expectantly.

"You crippled yourself because you stretched the rules till they broke. Simple as that."

Willie knows her line of thinking; it's a little like Cyril's, only further out. "But if there's *God* . . . I mean, I . . . didn't do anything . . . so bad."

"To have him cripple you?"

"Yeah."

"God didn't cripple you, Willie. *You* did. You stretched the rules till they broke; had to go a little faster than you could, push out there at the edge because you thought nothing could hurt you. You said that yourself."

"But . . . I didn't know."

"The rules don't slack off for naïveté," Lisa says. "Physics doesn't work on a sliding scale. You broke the rules, you got hurt." She nods a big nod. "So, now that you know why, how does that help?"

Willie shakes his head. "It doesn't."

"Might as well quit asking, then."

In Lisa's car, headed for the hospital, Willie tells her about Lacey.

"Don't know why you stay with him, Willie. Man's a pimp and that means he's dangerous. I've tried everything I know to get Angel away from him, but I've had no luck. She says she's got to stay with it another year till she gets out of school and can get a place. But I've known my share of whores, and you don't just get out when you want to."

"Think Lacey . . . won't let her out?"

"Would you turn Secretariat out to pasture three days before the Kentucky Derby because he said he didn't want to run?"

"Not . . . without a fight," Willie says.

"That's what I mean."

Lisa lets him out in front of the hospital and drives off; he'll take the bus from there. He finds Lacey sleeping and the doctor says they'll release him in the morning; wonders if Willie, or someone, will be there to pick him up.

Willie says he will and heads for the bus stop. He had hoped Lacey would be awake so they could talk about the living situation, but it will just have to wait.

At home he tries the number André gave him for Angel again, but there's no answer, so he heats up a can of chili on the stove and cranks up Bruce Springsteen on the sound system, pulling the shades in case he gets the urge to dance again. He does get the urge, so he sets the bowl on the coffee table and moves into the dining room. He can feel it; the same thing he felt on the court. He throws away moves he can't make, replaces them with ones he can. Somewhere down in there, maybe deep in his center, Willie can feel himself starting to come back. Tears fill his eyes as he realizes it's the first time since he got here that he thinks he may see his family again. But not yet.

— CHAPTER 16 —

"You're starting to look like a player," André says, popping one from twenty feet. Willie moves under the basket a little to the right for an unlikely rebound should André miss. He takes the ball out of the net and fires a hard one-handed bounce pass back; André, taking it on the move, pops another.

"Thanks," Willie says. "Actually, thanks to . . . Lisa. Boy, she never . . . gives up."

"Yeah," André agrees, "she's a good one. But she says you deserve all the credit. Says you been working your butt off."

"Only because . . . of what she'd do to me . . . if I didn't."

André laughs. "And best you don't forget it. Hey, Willie, you have friends back in Montana?"

"Yeah, I had friends."

"A lot, or a few?"

"A lot, I guess. Why?"

"I don't see you mix with kids much here. You work and you do your therapy with Lisa. But I don't see you with friends. Don't you ever get lonely?"

"Yeah, well, it's . . . a little lonely sometimes . . ."

"Having a hard time finding anyone you want to be close to?"

"Yeah," Willie admits. "A little, I . . . guess." Willie has been getting more and more comfortable with André over the past weeks, in the same way he felt close to Cyril. He doesn't feel that safety with other kids, though. Especially these kids. They're so tough. So grown-up.

André drives to the hoop, springs from the court as if in slow motion and slams the ball over the rim down into the net. It's effortless and Willie is envious. André sees his look. "Don't get to feeling sorry for yourself," he says. "You couldn't do that even if you hadn't whacked your bean. Listen, are you giving these kids a chance?"

"Actually," Willie says, popping in a jumper from about fifteen feet, "probably not. The only girl . . . I'm interested in works for the pimp . . . I'm living with, and the only guy I can beat in *any* athletic contest wants to be president . . . of the telephone company."

"That might not be true anymore," André says. "You should try to get into some pickup games out here. Lisa says you're coming along pretty fast. I'll bet you're better than you think."

Willie shrugs. André might be right. Something about this visualization Lisa has been working with him on has made his moves feel almost natural. He's starting to be able to see what's coming while he's wrapping up what's happening; it's working its way into a flow. He doesn't feel like the old Willie, but he feels like a *different* Willie and, as Lisa says, that's not all bad.

"And start hanging out with some of these kids," André says, taking his own shot out of the net and flipping it behind his back to Willie.

Willie catches it, parking it under his arm for a moment. "I don't . . . do any drugs," he says.

"So don't do any drugs. You think that's the only way you can get in at this school?"

Willie shrugs again. "There . . . are probably other ways, but . . . I don't know what they are."

"Then your job is to find out. But you can't find out if you don't put yourself out there."

Willie nods a big nod and fires a jumper from about twelve feet out on the baseline. It bounces straight back to him off the rim and he catches it, turning to go.

"Stop!" André hollers, pointing to the hoop. "Never leave the court on a miss. Never leave the court on anything but a swisher. Always go on a success."

Willie looks at him like André's crazy, but André only points again to the hoop. Willie fires two more from the same spot and the second one snaps the net.

André nods. "Better."

Willie finishes the polishing job on Lacey's car and leans over the hood, careful not to touch. "Like a mirror," he murmurs to himself, "only clearer." He won-

ders if he could be considered an accomplice to Lacey's
life for keeping the car looking so good, but decides
ladies probably don't go to work for a pimp just because
of how clean his car is. Besides, if Lacey didn't have to
feed Willie, he could have it done professionally every
week.

Lacey should be home soon. He had a morning-and-
afternoon route today and told Willie before he left he
wanted the car looking "like a fine piece of jewelry, jus'
sparklin' down the street" for this evening. They
haven't talked much since Lacey got out of the hospital
four weeks ago; just enough to let Willie know that
Lacey "done buried it, but jus' this once; no more."

The ringing phone pulls Willie's thoughts from Angel; she's back in school, but acts as if the night at
Lacey's never happened. The voice on the other end is
now familiar to Willie; Lacey's ex-wife. "Lemme talk to
Mr. Casteel." She says the name as if she's spitting out
raw sewage.

"He's . . . not here right now. Can I take a message?"

"Yeah, you can take a message," she says sarcastically.
"You tell Lacey his baby boy still rotting away in the
institution. Tell him what he done ain't never goin' go
away." A pause. "Who is this anyway?"

"My name's . . . Willie Weaver. I'm . . . staying
here for a while."

"Well, Willie Weaver, I don't know who you is, but if
you got a brain in you *head*, you best get away from Mr.
Lacey Casteel. He turn you life to heartache."

This is the first time Lacey's ex-wife has actually said
anything of substance to Willie and he doesn't know
how to respond. She sounds rough. "Would . . . you
like me to . . . have him call you?"

She laughs. "Tell you what, honey. You can have him call me all you want. Won't change nothin'. He won't call, an' even if he did, his baby still be rottin' away. An' for *that*, Mr. Lacey Casteel gonna rot in Hell." A loud click signals the end of the conversation.

Willie scribbles a short note on the miniature chalk-board he installed beside the phone for Lacey's messages: "Your ex called."

Sometime after midnight Willie hears fumbling with the outside lock. It takes longer than usual and he knows Lacey's drunk. He pretends to be asleep for a few seconds, but when it seems he's *never* going to get the key in, Willie gets up. Lacey's surprised when the door opens; stands swaying, eyes blood red, wondering how it opened magically, then spies Willie. "You don' have to get up," he slurs. "I woulda got it."

"That's okay," Willie says with a short laugh. "I had . . . to get up to . . . open the door anyway."

It slides over Lacey's head. Willie stands waiting while Lacey stares from the doorway. "You coming in?" he asks finally.

Lacey snaps to; stumbles through the door. Willie hasn't seen him this drunk. "Gone get me a beer," Lacey says, heading for the refrigerator.

Willie says, "That's . . . what you need," mostly to himself.

From the kitchen comes an anguished cry followed by something crashing against the sink. Usually when Lacey gets crazy, Willie makes himself invisible, but this time he walks to the kitchen door to check. Lacey doesn't seem mean tonight, just vulnerable. Willie sees the chalkboard lying on the floor, its message staring face up at them.

"Bitch!" Lacey screams. "Fat, nasty bitch! She tryin' kill me from inside!"

Willie slides back toward the living room to bed; let Lacey do whatever it takes to get this out of his system. He's told Willie enough times it's none of his "damn binnis" and Willie knows how fast Lacey turns mean.

"Wait," Lacey says before Willie can move even a few steps. "Time you know what all this shit about. Lacey gonna purge his soul. You be puttin' on your clothes, Chief. You an' me goin' for a ride." He grabs a half-full fifth of I. W. Harper whiskey from the cupboard and heads for the front door.

"I beat my boy," Lacey says in the car headed up Park Boulevard. "Beat 'im bad." He's sweating and continually wiping his eyes.

Willie's quiet. He looks to Lacey, then back to the bright white lines gliding under the Chrysler.

"Near to kill him," Lacey says. "Sometime I wish I had."

"You mean . . . like a son? You . . . have a son?"

"He barely a son now." Lacey's eyes cloud over and he grips the wheel hard. "Start on beatin' him. Couldn't stop. Beat my boy numb."

"You talking about your own kid?" For some reason, Willie's not comprehending. "You got a kid, Lacey?"

Lacey takes a long pull from the fifth. "Hell, yes, I'm talkin' 'bout a kid. What you *think* I'm talkin' about?"

Willie's quiet again, staring out at the street as they take the ramp to the freeway. Then, "Where're we going?"

"See my kid," Lacey says. "Gonna show you my kid."

"Where is he?"

"You jus' hold on. He still be there." Lacey grips the wheel even tighter. "He always be there."

By the time they reach Highland Hospital, Lacey is tight as a drum, sweat pouring off his forehead and down his temples, mixing with tears on his chin. Willie is afraid to speak, not so much for fear of making Lacey mad as because Lacey looks as if he might just blow apart. He doesn't think Lacey can talk—it's like he's spending his last ounce of energy just getting them there. Willie hasn't felt this uneasy since the night he tried to find his way to BART through the Oakland war zone.

Lacey pulls the Chrysler close to the curb about a block from the huge, dark institution and shuts down the lights. "Can't go in the front," he says. "Ain't allowed." He slams the car door. "Ain't allowed to see my boy; see what I done. Bitch had it made that way so she torture me res' of my life."

They turn up the side street next to the hospital, walk several yards along the ten-foot-high chain-link fence. In the blind spot between streetlights, Lacey stops and bends down, hands cupped, fingers interlaced.

"We . . . going over the fence?" Willie asks. "Won't we . . . get in trouble?"

"Could be," Lacey says, moving back and forth in his alcoholic sway. "Don' much matter."

Willie's been around Lacey long enough to know you don't argue when his mind's made up, which it always is, especially when he's drunk; so Willie drops his cane and steps into Lacey's makeshift sling, attempting to place his weight away from the arm with the wrist brace; the only visible remnant of that awful night with Lacey and Angel. Lacey pushes him high enough that Willie can grab the top frame of the fence and, with a little more shoving from below, pull himself over, dropping to the dark lawn on the other side. His cane lands beside him; then Lacey, stumbling as he hits the grass, pitching forward.

Lacey stands and brushes himself off, seemingly reaching down inside somewhere for dignity that may not be there, then marches straight toward the square brick building, Willie in tow.

They stop beneath a window too high to see into and Lacey grabs the steel drainpipe beside it like a gym rope, pulling himself up hand over hand until he's even with the window. Whatever pain he feels from the wrist is not evident. Willie hears a high moan, looks up to see Lacey's face go soft, his mouth and eyes fallen. Lacey stares a few more seconds through what looks to Willie to be bottomless despair, then drops back to the ground. "Go look," Lacey says in a voice so empty it wants to collapse. "He standin' direct across the room, lookin' right at the window. Don' worry, he don' see you."

"I can't get up that," Willie says, pointing to the pipe. "Only got . . . one good arm."

Lacey leans forward, placing his hands firmly just above his knees. "Stan' on my back."

Willie looks at Lacey's wrist brace, hesitates.

"Stan' on my goddam back!" Lacey hisses. He's wavering, but Willie walks around behind him, slips out of his shoes, placing his hands on Lacey's buttocks, and hops up on his back as if he were a circus rider mounting a horse. Carefully he moves his hands to Lacey's shoulderblades, attempting to stand. After a couple of slips, he's up, holding onto the window ledge for support. The room is dimly lit, and directly across from the window, exactly where Lacey said he'd be, stands a tall, extremely thin black boy; he could be anywhere from fifteen to forty. His long arms hang out of his plain white state-issue shirt like useless ebony twigs, their outstanding features the gnarled, twisted elbows and knuckles. Inside his head, Willie hears a voice: "Find your center" and realizes this boy doesn't have a center. He's staring at the window, but Willie can tell he doesn't see him. A narrow thread of spittle hangs from one side of his mouth, and as it lengthens, finally dropping to the floor, the boy makes no attempt to stop it. He's vacant; gone.

Willie is absolutely fixed on Lacey's son. He knows only the skeleton of the story behind all this, but, from his core, knows instantly this is *family* gone crazy. It comes in a flash: the boy before him is wrecked; the man beneath his feet, desperately holding on with everything he's got to stay just above the quicksand. This is what happens when we astonish ourselves with our capacity to be vicious; when we realize so late how our expectations have betrayed us. Suddenly he sees his father's face, and the hurt in his chest nearly drowns him.

The door next to the boy opens and Willie ducks, then peeks back over the ledge. The boy's body turns slowly, in a series of starts, to look at the nurse standing in the doorway, then back at the window. Below him, Willie feels through the soles of his feet the slow vibration of Lacey's sobs. Lacey wavers, steadies himself, then falls forward; Willie tumbling onto him. He lands with a hard thud, barely missing Lacey's head, and Lacey lies there, crying, pounding the grass weakly with one fist. Willie pulls himself up, reaches down to help Lacey, but Lacey tenses, holds tightly to the ground, face buried in the lawn. Willie stands staring down at him for nearly a full minute before saying, "Come on . . . Lacey. Let's go. I . . . saw him. I get it now."

With an audible sigh, almost a moan, Lacey pulls himself to his hands and knees. "He jus' there hauntin' me. He there an' I can't see him; they won't let me go close. But that bitch Coreen, she call me leas' once a day; tell me how I murder him. All she want be money. Long time I pay; but I never get to see him. Never get to make it right. She jus' call an' haunt me; tell me he a vegetable an' me a killer."

"And . . . you took me in to take his place."

Lacey's quiet a second, then says, "Yeah, you a cripple kid. I get this idea to get me out of Hell. Raise me a white cripple kid. Can't fix all the bad shit, but maybe I make up *some.*"

"Let's . . . go back home," Willie says.

Lacey stands, the effects of the alcohol washed out of his body by a dynamite blast of anguish.

Willie's perched on the edge of the concrete wall bordering the patio next to the school, surrounded by schoolmates and feeling somewhat lost. He doesn't know what to say; how to get in. The day is warm, even hot for March; the bay fog burned off early. Most of the boys have removed their shirts; some are just coming from a lunchtime game on the court, and Willie looks around in envy. He's not even sure he knows what he looks like anymore, it's been so long since he's been willing to look. He used to like his body; be proud of his hard, natural, well-muscled build. But now he's lopsided; his left arm and leg are noticeably smaller, and he's very self-conscious about letting anyone see him. He catches a glimpse of Angel sitting on the grass talking to some other girls, and his envy of these guys intensifies. He wants to take off his shirt and show off some of his old moves on the court. He looks behind him to see Warren Hawkins lighting up a joint. Immediately Willie feels self-conscious; like he's in for trouble. Warren is big time at OMLC; everybody's hero. He's a tall, fast, strong black kid; real smart—though that isn't borne out on his report card—with the build of a racehorse and these lightning-quick eyes that miss nothing. Everyone knows he's a fighter and everyone knows his temper is like quicksilver. He's easygoing most of the time, with a good sense of humor; really appealing; a natural leader. It's a bad idea to get on Warren's bad side.

Warren tokes the joint and passes it on, and Willie fidgets a little. "You be watchin' right around that corner there," Warren says to Willie. "That be where André my man comin' from if he comin'. You give me a signal, I be havin' this roach for lunch."

Willie nods uneasily, knowing he'd be off the face of the earth if he refused, but feeling an allegiance to André. He hopes the joint will be smoked before it gets to him, but it isn't and he nonchalantly passes it on. Warren glances up. "You passin' up some good shit," he says and there's an undertone of suspicion.

Willie smiles and says, "Yeah. Can't . . . do any dope since I . . . got hurt."

Warren nods. "You ain't no narc." It's a question.

Willie shakes his head. "Nope. Just can't do dope."

"Narc last this long," Warren says, snapping his fingers. "One second he awake, then he asleep."

"I'm . . . not a narc," Willie says again, calmly, his heart thundering in his throat.

"Awake. Asleep," Warren says again, snapping his fingers.

A short, stocky black kid who hangs with Warren all

the time—Willie knows him only as Kato—lights up another joint and hands it to Warren. "Come on, man, he ain't no narc. You jus' smokin' too much this good weed, make you crazy with par-a-noia. Tha's a brain disease you get when you become a drug addict like you is, Hawk."

"Shee. I ain't no addict. *You* the addict. You ain't been down since Jimmy Carter runnin' things."

"Who Jimmy Carter?"

"So, Willie Weaver," Hawk says. "André the Terrible say you about ready to shoot some hoops with the big boys, that right?"

Willie shrugs. "Sometime," he says. "Been working at getting it back."

"André say you pretty hot shit where you come from, up there in Montana."

"Where men be men," Kato says, "an' sheep be *nervous.*"

"Whooo. Tha's a good one," Hawk laughs. "Tha's *cold,* Kato. Make fun of a man's *home*land."

Willie laughs. He hasn't heard that one.

"Anyway," Hawk says. "You come on out when you ready. Old Hawk show you some *moves.*"

"I've . . . been watching," Willie says. "You've already shown me some moves."

"Shee," Kato says. "Easy to have moves when you six-five an' built swift. Come out an see some of *my* moves. Show you some rollin', bowlin' moves Hawk only dream of." He turns to Hawk. "I done what I said. Checked my wheels out against BART."

Hawk looks puzzled. "What you talkin' 'bout?"

"Tryin' to see what's the fastest way to school. Rode my bike one day, took BART the next. Bike one day,

BART the next. Get *down*, Ka-to. Alter*nate*. Did that for a week."

Everyone looks at Kato like So The Hell What?

"Know what I fin' out?"

"What you fin' out, Kato?"

"Take me less time to ride my bike. Every day. Really. Fin' out BART be worse than my bike." Kato convulses into a high laughter, as Willie's head snaps up. "Get it?" Kato chokes. "BART be worse than my bike. Like a dog."

Hawk slips Kato into a headlock and makes him promise "no more them jive-ass things." "Pigs come get you for that," he says.

Willie relaxes and laughs. Awful as it seems, this may be the connection between his worlds.

— CHAPTER 17 —

For a time following the night outside Lacey's battered son's room, things seem to quiet down a bit for Willie. He becomes more a part of the group that hangs around Hawk and Kato, though he doesn't find *real* closeness, and concentrates hard in school and harder at regaining his physical self.

Lisa is great. "Tell Lacey we need a hundred and forty dollars for a special class that isn't covered by your scholarship," she says as they finish their workout on the court, ripping the Velcro fastener off her small wrist weight and flipping it into the backseat of her car. They've worked eight weeks, and she's removed a lot of the extra weights to match Willie's improvement; only these small ones remain.

"A hundred and forty dollars," Willie said. "For what?"

Lisa smiles. "I won't tell you, then you won't have to tell him. Tell him it's a hell of a deal, though. Normal cost would be about two hundred and fifty dollars. Tell him all the kids taking the class have to pay extra. *Don't* tell him you're the only one taking it." She walks around to the driver's side, opens the door, leans her elbows easily on the roof. "And get ready to clear out some early-morning time, say around six. It's time for Phase Two."

Willie doesn't question her; he's come to trust her completely, knowing she keeps her little secrets and surprises to spring on him so he won't have time to figure out reasons and excuses.

He stays on the court after she drives away, working on a move to his left that requires only one dribble with his left hand and a long step; designed to keep honest any defenders cheating to his right because he is so obviously right-sided. He dribbles several times with his right hand, visualizing a defender in his path to the basket, cross-dribbles to his left, taking a long step around, then back to his right hand, moving in under the hoop, protecting the ball with his body, flipping it up for a reverse lay-up. He attempts the move ten times, scores eight.

"Not bad for a man be earthbound."

Willie turns to see Hawk and Kato and a guy he doesn't know walking through the gate toward the court, and waves. The edge is off his relationship with Hawk—Hawk knows now he isn't a narc—but Willie's still pretty careful; partly because when he watches

Hawk play he wishes desperately he could match skills
with him back when he was healthy. If only Hawk
knew, if he had seen him at the Crazy Horse Electric
game, Willie would get the respect he deserves.

"Little two-on-two?" Kato says, popping a jumper
from the free-throw line.

"Naw, I . . . gotta go."

Hawk says, "Let it wait. Time you see what you can
do. Time to take all you new guns to the war. See if they
shoot. See if you got *ammo.*"

Willie starts to protest, but Hawk says, "Me an' you,
Crazy Horse. You take my man Kato. I take Ernie. Do or
die." He swishes one from the top of the key, turning to
walk to the half line even before the ball snaps through
the net, waiting patiently there while Ernie removes
his sweats. Ernie is about an inch taller and a bit stockier
than Hawk. They look to be a good match. Ernie doesn't
speak, just bends down, grabbing his toes to stretch,
then walks toward the basket, taking two long, quick
strides, and leaps easily to the rim, hanging there a few
seconds before dropping to the ground.

"Ernie think he bust up the rim, won' have to suffer
no *humiliation,*" Hawk laughs, flipping the ball to Willie, signaling the start of action. Kato crowds him and
Willie dribbles to his right, protecting the ball with his
body. Kato's hand flicks around Willie like a snake's
tongue, but Willie's long arm keeps it away. With preci-
sion timing, as the snake's tongue retracts, he flips the
ball around behind Kato's back into the key, just as
Hawk breaks around Ernie, and Hawk scoops it up at
full speed, faking once, then sliding behind Ernie, who
has overplayed him. He lays it up easily for the point.
They score four more before turning the ball over; one

of them on Willie's short jumper and another on a sort of jump-hook he developed to keep leapers away.

Kato and Ernie catch up on Ernie's sweet outside baseline jumper and a couple of lightning-quick moves to the hoop that leave Hawk a step behind. Kato gets around Willie for two easy ones, but Willie adjusts and eventually is able to keep him outside most of the time. Excitement floods through him at being able to stay with these guys, though most of his contribution comes through pinpoint passes to Hawk, working the inside against Ernie. His old anticipation is coming back—he almost always knows where Hawk is going to be. Occasionally he gets excited and throws the ball away, but each time that happens he slows down, closing his eyes; centering himself, remembering the miles of tape Lisa has shown him of Larry Bird "taking whatever time he needs to make his move," no matter what the skills of his opponent. And Willie gets back in control. He wishes Lisa had stayed to watch.

They play four games to fifteen; Willie can't even remember who wins which. He just knows he's back doing something he loves; something he thought was gone from his life.

"A hunnert forty bucks for what?" Lacey looks at him as if he's asked to drive the Chrysler to Montana.

"I'm not sure. Some kind of special class. Both Lisa and André say it's required."

"Other kids all payin'?"

Willie nods. "Lisa says everyone who takes it has to pay, and that it's a required class for me."

"Jus' thinkin' some new ways to suck old Lacey dry," Lacey says in disgust. "Hunnert an' forty bucks. You gonna be doin' some *work* around here for that. Maybe build me a hot tub."

Willie laughs. "Lacey, I'll make you a deal. If you don't have five hundred dollars rolled up in your front pocket right this minute, I will build you a hot tub. If you do, I get the money free. A gift."

"Cold day you get a hunnert forty from Lacey Casteel as a *gift,"* Lacey says. "You gonna *work* for this."

" 'Tote that barge; lift that bale,' " Willie sings.

Lacey reaches into his front pocket and peels off a hundred forty in twenties and tens. "You in *deep* financial difficulties now, boy, an' don't you be forgettin'."

"Thanks, Lacey. I won't be forgettin'. Really. Thanks."

Two days later Lisa drives Willie through downtown Oakland and under the Oakland estuary to Alameda, a nine-minute drive from school, to Nautilus of Alameda, where she plunks down the $140 cash to take advantage of a special membership drive. She also buys one for herself. Then she walks him through all the weight machines, showing him special ways to work on his left side to catch it up as far as possible. After that, three times a week—Monday, Wednesday and Friday—she packs him into her car the moment school lets out—before he starts his janitorial duties—and hauls him off to Nautilus to work out for an hour and a half. And Willie gets stronger.

That same afternoon Lisa drives him to an old building surrounded by more old buildings with steel bars guarding what few windows aren't already boarded over. Inside, they watch for more than a half-hour as a young Japanese man in a World War II crew cut—tiny in stature, but catlike in quickness and anticipation—guides fifteen pre-teen and teenage kids through what looks to Willie like a cross between some kind of Oriental martial art and poetry.

"It's called Tai Chi," Lisa whispers as the three rows of kids glide through their movements. Willie's really drawn to them because it looks like they have an abundance of what he's been missing: balance. The instructor looks up and spots Lisa, nods calmly, almost serenely, and continues the exercises. When he finally approaches them, almost gliding across the floor as if walking and flying are the same, Willie expects a bow followed by some wise utterance *à la* David Carradine in "Kung Fu."

"Lisa, you hot little number," the instructor says in perfect English. "Where you been? I thought we were going to start working out again a month ago. I've been lusting for you."

"Hi, Sammy. I know. I've just been really busy. This is Willie Weaver, the boy I told you about."

"Ah," Sammy says, "Crazy Horse." He puts out his hand and Willie takes it, smiling self-consciously. "I've been expecting you. Lisa thinks I can help re-design your unit and then we'll all be famous when she sells her thesis to the *Enquirer.*"

Lisa laughs. " 'How I Regained Use of My Arms and Legs on a Simple Diet of Beefalo Patties and Carrot Stix.' I'll write it under the name of Victoria Principal."

"So," Sammy says, "how about next week? Start about six Monday morning? Work at least four days?"

Lisa nods. "That okay with you, Willie?"

Willie's along for the ride. Lisa's never steered him wrong yet. "Fine."

"I'd put you in a class," Sammy says, "but I don't want to limit which disciplines we use. Tai Chi isn't enough. I want to make this as intensive and varied as we need to.

I haven't worked with physical disabilities before, but it seems like a perfect thing to do. Besides, it gives me a chance to watch Lisa in her tights." He nods back to the kids exercising across the room. "Wouldn't do for them to see my Oriental mystique broken down." He kisses Lisa a quick, soft kiss on the mouth that tells Willie there's more going on here than just a thesis, and pads back to his class. As Willie and Lisa start for the door, Sammy hollers back at them, "And bring your cane!"

"Listen to Sammy real close," Lisa says, driving back toward the school so Willie can finish his janitorial duties. "He teases a lot, but he says damn little that's meaningless. Everything he'll say to you is something you can use; either now or sometime."

"You like him," Willie says.

"I do like him. And I love him. Someday, when our paces match . . ."

In the following months Sammy taps into Willie in a way that almost frightens him. Willie discovers that his mind and body are merely extensions of each other, and Sammy teaches him how one can transfer power to the other. He learns that, even though he is just less than six feet tall, there is a bottomless well inside him, holding a map with specific directions around his physical limitations, information about his emotional pain that helps him let it be. He sometimes finds himself telling Sammy his best-kept secrets in the same way he might talk about what he's going to have for lunch; realizing only later, lying flat on his makeshift bed at Lacey's house, what he has revealed. And he knows, in that way that humans sometimes just know things, that Sammy would never hurt him with any of what he has disclosed.

And Sammy teaches him to use the cane. "I don't want to make you a warrior," he says, "but I also don't want you helpless on the street at a bus stop. Ever." So Willie incorporates the cane into his balance.

On a hot day in July, a day when the natural air-conditioning of the Bay Area is on the fritz and the fog stands far out to sea, Lisa and Sammy and Willie sit in a circle, cooling down after a tough workout.

"So, where are you, Willie?" Sammy asks. "Where do you want to go now?"

Willie shrugs, thinking.

"What's in you that needs work?"

Willie can't get it.

"What hurts?"

"My family," he says. "My sister. My goddam sister . . ."

"Your sister's gone."

Willie nods. "I know. But it doesn't leave me alone."

"It probably never will," Sammy says. "But you'll find a place to put it. What else?"

"There's one thing," Willie says, "and I know it shouldn't be there. I should just be glad to be playing sports again. I mean, when we play ball at the park, I'm good, I really am. I play smart and I never hurt my team. I get my points; almost never throw the ball away."

"And?"

"And then I go home and I replay the Crazy Horse Electric game in my head, and I know I'll never have that *moment* again. It was *so* high. Everything was together. And I begin to wish it hadn't happened; like if I didn't know about it, I wouldn't miss it so much. It's so selfish . . ." His voice trails off, then snaps back. "It's like with Missy. Sometimes I wish she'd never been born, just so I wouldn't know how special it was to have her . . ."

"You can choose to look at that lots of ways," Sammy says. "You can use your sister—or the baseball game—to beat you down or build you up. But remember: every moment of your life is part of you. You say you can never have that moment, or your sister, again. I say you'll always have them. They're part of what makes you Willie Weaver."

Lisa massages the back of Sammy's neck, running her hands through his short hair and down over his chest, toward the elastic band of his gym shorts, and Sammy smiles. He leans over and reaches for the wallet inside his workout pants on the floor beside them, pulling out a five-dollar bill; hands it to Willie. "Why don't you go get yourself some breakfast for about forty-five minutes?" he says, and Willie leaves them alone.

In late August, after a basketball workout with Lisa and a couple of pickup games with some neighborhood stars, Lisa calls Willie into the office, once again booting André, who is trying to come up with the fall class schedule, outside. "Close your eyes," she says, and Willie obeys. "Extend your arms and touch your fingers together lightly," and again Willie does as he's told. "Now bring your fingers to your center." Willie's center has moved.

When school starts in September, Willie sees it with new eyes; he's feeling power over his life. On registration day he notices Angel standing in line to register for Chemistry, starts toward her, stops, then goes ahead. He's not had any kind of meaningful dialogue with her since that crazy night at Lacey's, but she hasn't been off his mind for more than the length of one pickup basketball game. And if Willie knows anything, it's that you'd better act when you get the chance; because once the chance is gone, it may be gone forever.

"How you doing?" he asks, sliding into line behind her.

"Okay." She's polite; a little cool.

Willie's quiet a moment, looking for a way in. Angel doesn't offer one. "S'pose we could have lunch?" he asks. "I'd like to talk."

"About what?"

"I don't know. Stuff."

"Lunch here?" she asks, pointing around the cafeteria, which has been converted for the day to the registration room. "I don't think there's lunch today. We're out at noon."

"No, not here. We could go over to the mall. Have our choice."

Angel looks slightly annoyed, but sighs and says, "Sure, why not? Meet you out front by the gate a little after twelve."

"You still working for Lacey?" Willie asks over his bacon burger. "I mean, you still . . ."

"Yeah, I'm still working for him."

Willie's quiet. That's as far as the conversation has gotten in his head. He wants to ask why she doesn't quit, now that he got Lacey to agree to let that happen; the result of a marathon argument the night after they saw Lacey's son at Highland; Willie would stay if Lacey agreed to let Angel off the hook. Lacey did agree—too easily, as if he knew something Willie did not. Two weeks later Willie asked him about it and Lacey just said, "I tol' her," and shrugged. Willie had been afraid to ask Angel about it, mostly because of his gut feeling that Lacey actually did offer and Angel declined.

He's still afraid to ask, but does anyway. "Did Lacey tell you what we talked about?"

Angel plays dumb.

"Last year. After the fight."

Angel looks away, then down at her plate. She doesn't answer.

"He did tell you."

"He told me."

"Well?"

"Well, what?"

"Are you going to quit?" Willie's insides are churning in response to the head movies he always gets when he brings this up. He knows what prostitutes do, and his imagination won't leave it alone.

Angel's answer is restrained. "No, I'm not going to quit."

The right words won't come. He wants to tell her he's concerned for her; that he cares for her; wants her life to be better. Instead: "Why not?"

Angel takes a deep breath. "What are you, my daddy?"

He leans back. "No, I'm not your daddy. I just . . . Well, I just can't get you out of my head. I can't stand it that you're a . . . well, that you work for Lacey, and I can't stand not spending time with you."

"I'm a whore, Willie."

"I know. But Lacey said he'd let you off the hook."

"You think I'm a whore because of Lacey? If Lacey wasn't my pimp, I'd get someone else. I'm a whore because that's how I survive. I *wanna* be a whore, okay? So leave it alone."

Willie blows. "So you gonna do that crap all your life? Why you bother going to school? You don't have to go to school to be a whore. Shit, look at all the time you're wasting. Six hours a day. How many guys is that?"

Angel gets up to leave.

"Wait. I'm sorry. It's none of my business. I just can't help it. I really care about you."

"You really care about me. Shit. You want what every man wants. You want into my pants. You're just a little sweeter about it."

Willie's embarrassed. "No, really. That's not it. I really care about you."

"How could you care about me? You don't even know me. You don't know *nothin'* about me. You couldn't. No one does. You care about my skin and my body and what I can do."

Willie knows she's right, in part. He *doesn't* know anything about her. But he's so attracted it aches. It *has* to be more than just wanting sex. "If I just wanted sex," he tries, "why does it bother me so much that you're with other guys? If I just wanted sex, I wouldn't care. I'd just save up my money and come find you."

"Look, Willie," Angel says patiently. "Don't play word games with me. You know what you know and I know what I know. You know how girls get to be whores? Girls get to be whores when they grow up thinking sex is the only way to get anything. You know when I had sex first? Seven years old. My uncle. Till I was seventeen. It was ugly and I hated it, but he was nice to me and he gave me things I'd never have gotten any other way. It doesn't matter whether you care about me or not. Nothing's going to change. Now, do you want me to pay for this lunch? I probably make a whole lot more money than you do."

"No," Willie says, defeated. "I can pay for lunch."

— CHAPTER 18 —

Weekends during the first two months of school, André, Lisa, Willie and anyone they can recruit paint the school building. OMLC starts to take on the look of the castle André envisioned, and they work like demons, taking breaks for three-on-three games with neighborhood stars and barbecued chicken and ribs and burgers that André cooks on his portable hibachi. Willie, under Lisa's constant "guidance," works as much as possible with his left hand. Sometimes her guidance includes tying his right hand to his belt.

These are wonderful, relaxed days for Willie. He loves being part of whatever club it is that André and Lisa belong to; the days have been sunny and warm, for the Bay, and he's getting strong and tan and confident. Sometimes Sammy comes to help and he always does the hard places, hanging upside down off the roof to paint under the eaves and threatening to drop on his head and splatter if Lisa won't take five quick minutes to run into the thick shrubbery behind the building with him. "I know you," she says. "What'll we do with the other four minutes?"

Sammy giggles his high giggle and paints away like a madman, moving along the roof like a cat, singing a song he obviously made up called, "Shoulda Been a Sherpa."

Some days kids from the school come and paint, but more often than not they work for about a half-hour, spending the rest of the afternoon shooting hoop and eating whatever André cooks. Except for Telephone

Man. Telephone Man comes to work; and though he moves pretty slow and gets paint on a lot of windows, he contributes, staring closely at his work, talking to his scraper or his brush about the infinite number of "chickenshit rip-offs" that exist in his universe. André usually gives him an area of his own to work on, promising a small memorial plaque to let future generations of OMLC know Telephone Man's part in beautifying their school.

On a Saturday in late October, when the outside work is nearly finished, Willie lets himself into the building early in the morning to polish the floors. He unlocks the student-lounge door so he can get the floor polisher out of the storeroom located just off the kitchen, and freezes. Scrawled in black spray paint on the off-white wall, probably four feet high and six feet long, is JO BOYS. Willie's heart instantly leaps into his throat and he hurries around the building, checking the entrances and exits. All locked. *How did they get in?* He rushes down the stairs to the basement and sees the logo again on the staircase, and again scrawled across one complete wall in the open room in the basement. He checks the entrances once more, thinking maybe one was left ajar, but now he'll never know because he's pulled them all tight. The sight of the name sends chills shooting through him and he gets the extra paint out of the storeroom to cover it, knowing it won't do a lot of good if they have a way in, but just wanting it gone. His heart settles some by the time he's painted everything over, and he continues with the floors, telling himself that most likely the panic bar on one of the doors was down and all he needs to do is be sure everything is tight when he leaves in the evenings. His mind tells him there's no way those guys would remember him or know where he was if they did, but his paranoia says they've followed him and want to put him away for some reason.

He decides to have lunch at the mall and uses the shortcut down the steep concrete stairway from Kempton to Broadway, avoiding the tougher section of the neighborhood, as he usually does. A half-block from the stairway he looks up to see a sight equally as chilling to him as the message sprayed on the school walls. It's Kam—has to be—spinning and kicking, spinning and kicking on the concrete bench at the top of the stairway. His buddies are cheering him on, almost absentmindedly, laughing and slapping each other around, looking bored; dangerous. They've noticed Willie coming and Willie feels he can't turn around, let them smell his fear; so he walks on toward them, avoiding eye contact. For a moment he thinks it's over when they leave no room to pass and none of them makes space, but after a tense five seconds Willie mumbles, "Excuse me" and they move aside. Kam stops; watches him. Willie thinks he notices the cane—*recognizes* the cane—but can't be sure. Descending the steps, he holds his breath, listening for footsteps, but the voices get fainter and fainter, and by the time he's at the bottom, Willie feels he's cheated death. He stops, closing his eyes. They still look young, and they still look scary. Especially Kam, with his cold, vacant stare; he looks like a guy with nothing to lose.

On Sunday, Willie takes the bus up to school just to check the place out; hoping—silently *chanting* inside— that the Jo Boys couldn't or didn't get in. His heart sinks when he opens the lounge door to see their name freshly sprayed again over his repair work. Again he checks the windows and doors, but everything's locked tight.

He's frustrated and angry and for the first time he wonders just how tough this Kam really is. Before, when Kam wasted him, Willie was scared and crippled, but he doesn't feel crippled anymore and now his cane isn't just something to walk with; not since Sammy showed him all the things it can be used for in a pinch. He leaves the slogan on the walls for André and the rest of the school to see tomorrow. Hawk just might have feelings about some punks sneaking in to mess up "his place"; and maybe the contacts to do something about it.

When André sees the Jo Boys' handiwork on Monday morning, he immediately calls the police, with whom he has an intimate relationship, partly from the nature of the school itself and partly because one of the men assigned to patrol the area has two kids enrolled. Willie walks into the office in the middle of André's conversation with him, a thick, quiet fireplug of a man named Maurice.

". . . goes up into the prison system," Maurice is saying, as André listens intently. "See, they recruit these gang kids as young as they can. Then if they want a felony done on the outside, they get one of them to do it because the law usually won't do much more than put them away for a few months at most; particularly if they don't have priors. And when I'm talking felony, I'm talking anything from assault to robbery to murder." He leans forward. "I don't want to make you nervous, André, but I've taken some awful big guns away from some awful little kids."

André shakes his head in disbelief, but he's lived in

this town long enough to believe. "So what happens, we just let them run loose?"

"Not necessarily," Maurice says. "They're tough, but they're still kids. Sometimes we can scare them. If they don't have a beef with someone here—any reason for revenge—sometimes we can make it worth it for them to leave things alone. Roust 'em. Ship 'em off for a few days. Make deals."

"Well, I don't *think* they have a beef with anyone here," André says. "I haven't even heard them mentioned other than the time they beat up Willie here, but that was before he was a student. 'Course I don't hear everything that goes down in drug deals."

At Maurice's request, Willie goes over the incident at the bus stop his first night in town, and Maurice is convinced it has nothing to do with the current problem. He gets up to leave. "Well, see what you can find out, but make sure your kids know not to escalate things. We'll do what we can."

"I'll do what I can, too," André says. "But I don't know how much control I'll have over some of my kids if they think they're being held hostage by a bunch of punks. I've got some fighters here."

Maurice says, "Don't I know it," as he disappears through the door.

"That's all I need," André says. "I can hear me telling a guy like Warren Hawkins I want him to lie low while these guys trash our place."

Willie nods. He knows André's like a rudder here; guiding from behind, watching which way the river's going at all times; helping kids do their best in the direction they're already headed because he knows too much has already gone on in their lives for him to be able to change the course of that river. He uses a heavy hand once in a while, but not often, and if this stuff with the Jo Boys blows up, André might not be able to stop it. Street law is street law.

Telephone Man slithers in the office door, hugging close to the wall, and drops a note on André's desk. "From my mom," he says in his deep bass voice. "Don't read it till I leave."

"Stay where you are," André says, opening it. He frowns. "It says there's a box of Bisquick missing from your kitchen," and Telephone Man nods.

"So what about it?" André asks.

Telephone Man shrugs.

"Does she think you took it?"

Telephone Man shrugs again.

"Did you?"

Telephone Man hesitates, looking at the ground. He shakes his head. "No."

"So why did your mom send me this note?" André asks.

Telephone Man shrugs again, palms up.

"Okay," André says, "go to class. I'll call your mom."

Telephone Man disappears around the door jamb and is gone, Willie watching in wonder.

Willie looks up to André. "What was that?"

André laughs. "I don't know. His parents aren't without their strangeness either. Jack didn't get that way on his own. Sometimes when they fight with him about something, they threaten to tell me and he straightens up. They don't have much control over him. Hell, they don't know what to control." He shakes his head. "Listen, if you see him with a box of Bisquick any time today, let me know, okay?"

"Won't let him out of my sight," Willie teases.

* * *

In the English room, just before first period, Hawk holds court. "Them China boys come in here one more time, get me some silky black scalps," he says. "I be seein' that karate boy flippin' his feet around like he some kinda hot shit, but he mess with the Hawk, I put him a-*way*."

Mr. Sauer, the English teacher, enters and listens a few minutes, then says, "Why don't we just wait and see what happens? No sense getting all dressed up if there's no place to go." André has obviously talked with the teachers and told them to downplay things as much as possible—avoid giving guys like Hawk a good reason to get cranked up.

"Oh," Hawk says, "I wait an' see, all right. But don' *be* no punk China boys messin' up my place. Get they heads fixed."

"I didn't realize you cared so much, Mr. Hawkins," Mr. Sauer says. "I mean, judging by the number of holes you've put in things around here . . ."

Hawk looks down. "Ain't done that in a while," he says, almost apologetically. " 'Sides, it's one thing when you mess up you own place; somethin' else when some-one else does it."

"I suppose that's true," Mr. Sauer says. "At any rate, let's develop a patient attitude, okay?"

As Hawk shrugs, Telephone Man enters the room, holding his stomach, and slides into his desk near the rear of the room, next to the door, unnoticed. Halfway through class he slips out again the same way he came.

Willie feels tremendous relief when the buzzer rings to end class. He knew he had to go to the bathroom a half-hour before class started, but kept putting it off for one reason or another and then class started and he had to wait. Stuffing his books carelessly into his pack, he heads to the rest room. He bursts through the door into a war zone. The walls and ceiling are spackled with a reddish-brown substance vaguely resembling cookie dough, but smelling of human waste and strawberries. Through the open door of one stall he sees the toilet stuffed with clothes; Telephone Man's clothes; and huddled in the middle of the floor, stark raving naked, squats Telephone Man himself, rocking, shivering; staring straight ahead.

"Hey, Jack, man, you okay?"

Telephone Man doesn't answer, but his lower lip quivers. Beside him, speckled with whatever it is that covers the rest of the room, sits his half-open book bag. Willie looks inside; reaches in to pull out an empty box of Bisquick. "This what your mom was looking for?" Willie asks.

Telephone Man nods, his lower lip quivering more. Willie digs deeper into the bag and comes out with an empty plastic bottle of strawberry-scented shampoo. The chemistry of what has happened flashes in his head, and Willie turns away, clamping his hand over his mouth to cut off a burst of laughter. At best, Telephone Man's eating habits are horrid, and he *can't read*. He must've eaten the Bisquick on the way to school, then found the shampoo in the restroom when he got here. It's Willie's; or it was. He keeps it here for times when he showers at school because his time is so short. Telephone Man must've thought he'd run into a big bottle of Smucker's surprise.

"Hey, Jack, man, you really okay now?"

Telephone Man nods and wraps his arms tighter around his shoulders.

"It's okay, man. Really," Willie says. "Listen, you stay

right here and I'll go get you some clothes from Lost and Found. I'm gonna lock the door, okay? So nobody will come in."

Telephone Man nods, and starts to cry; a silent cry from deep, deep down inside. The cry of one more humiliation.

Willie squats down beside him and puts his hands on his shoulders. "Hey, come on," he says. "No one's gonna find out, okay? I'll tell everyone the toilets are plugged and they can't come in. They'll just have to use the girls' can. I'll get you out of here as soon as class starts. No one will know. Really. Promise." Willie shakes him gently. "Okay?"

Telephone Man is still crying, but he nods, and as Willie leaves he padlocks the ancient free-swinging door from the outside, scrawling OUT OF ORDER on a piece of notebook paper and sticking it to the door with a piece of gum. On his way down the hall, he says loudly, "Men's can is out of order. You'd be *real* sorry if you went in there. Use the girls' can."

In the office, Willie almost splits a gut telling André. "You can't tell anyone, though," he says. "I promised."

"Are you sure he's okay? Physically, I mean?"

"I think so," Willie says. "There couldn't be any left in him. You'll know what I mean when you see it." He gets a sweatshirt and a pair of pants from Lost and Found as he hears the buzzer for second period.

"Tell him I'll give him a ride home," André says. "He doesn't live very far."

"Actually, I think I'll point him toward the bus," Willie says. "He really needs to think no one else knows."

"Whatever you think. Just be sure he's okay."

Telephone Man is okay. By the time Willie's back, he's out of his crouched position and staring into the toilet where he stuffed his clothes. Willie knocks quietly, whispering, "It's me," through the door before unlocking the lock. "Here, put these on," he says. "You can run home and change and be back before noon. I'll keep it locked up until I can hose it out." He looks over Telephone Man's shoulder into the toilet. "How come you put them there?"

"Thought I could flush 'em down," Telephone Man booms. "Got shit all over 'em. Chickenshit rip-off, if you ask me."

Willie marvels at how fast he's bounced back. "Looks like a chickenshit rip-off to me," Willie says. Then, "You sure you're feeling okay, now? Be able to go home and come back? I mean, you're not still sick, are you?"

"I'm okay. You just don't tell, okay? Promise you won't tell."

"I already promised, Jack. I won't tell."

Telephone Man looks him straight in the eye for a moment, seems satisfied, and nods his big nod. Willie sticks his head out the door into the hall, looks both ways to be sure it's empty and gently nudges Telephone Man out. "Hustle back," he says. "No one will even know you were gone if you hurry."

Telephone Man slides along the wall to the door and is gone. Willie locks the door to the rest room and heads for Government class.

"They've got Telephone Man! They're beating him up! Down by the stairs! Somebody better come quick! They're hurting him bad!"

Hawk is out of his desk in a second, leaps over two more and flies into the hall past Yolanda Duke, the freshman girl delivering the message. Kato is close behind, and the room empties. Hawk shoots out the front gate and down the sidewalk toward the stairs before most of the rest clear the building. Willie turns the corner in time to see Hawk jump over Telephone Man lying on the ground next to the concrete bench and sprint down the stairs two and three at a time. At the bottom he is on Kam before Kam has time to turn and fight, slamming him down face first, grabbing a handful of hair; driving his face into the gravel next to the street.

"Done messed up this time, China boy," Hawk hisses into his ear, then pushes harder.

Kam struggles and Hawk pulls his head back hard. Kam struggles again and Hawk's knee rams into the back of his leg; Kam stifles a scream. "That how you China boys do you stuff?" Hawk asks. "Beatin' on dummies? You better hope he ain' hurt bad, or I gonna grind you face right off you head."

"Hey, man," Kam says. "We didn't know who he was. We were just roughin' him up a little for some bread, man. He's not hurt."

"You *hope* he ain't, you mean."

Hawk twists around to look back up the stairs and as he does Kam scrambles to get away. Hawk's knee slams hard into the middle of Kam's back as André runs down the stairs toward them.

Hawk puts his mouth close to Kam's ear before André can get to them and says, "Tha's my school. You stay away from my school. You don' be puttin' you shitty little China-boy writin' all over it and you don' be even *lookin'* at nobody goes to school there. Understand? Are you compre-*hend*-ing what I sayin'?"

"Yeah," Kam says through gritted teeth, "I understand."

"I'm gettin' up now," Hawk says, loosening his hold slowly. "You try any that fancy foot shit, I'll embarrass

you, front of you friends. Then I'll beat you up *bad.*"
Hawk lets go of Kam's hair and slowly removes his knee
from the middle of his back.

André is there, but sees Hawk letting the kid up and
stands back. At the top of the stairs, Willie and most of
the rest of the class are checking out Telephone Man,
who has a bloody lip and swollen eye but, other than
that, is just dazed and scared. He isn't talking, not even
crying; just breathing very short and staring; shudder-
ing. They pick him up and help him back to school.

At lunchtime, on the patio, Hawk approaches Willie.
"China boys gonna be back," he says.

Willie winces. "How do you know?"

"They think they a gang," Hawk says. "That boy be
embarrassed. They be back."

Willie's not sure why Hawk's telling him this. "So
what do we do? Why you telling me?"

. "You got the keys to this place. We come up here
tonight and wait for them. We sit in the dark and jus'
wait. They got to learn. We don' teach 'em, they don'
learn. Can't tell André. You can give me the keys or
come up with us."

The idea of spending the night in the school building
isn't appealing, but Willie immediately recognizes he's
in a pinch. If he tells André, he's on Hawk's list. If he
gives up his keys and André finds out, he couldn't face
him.

"Didn't you say them China boys done you bad at the
bus stop?" Hawk asks, reading Willie's mind.

Willie nods. "Yeah."

"Well, what go 'round come 'round. This you chance
to be a cowboy."

Willie's resigned. "What time?"

CHAPTER 19

Willie looks at his watch and moves uncomfortably on the old couch they brought down to the basement room from the student lounge. Hawk and Kato are more than an hour late. That makes no sense because Hawk was so pumped up Willie didn't think he'd go home for dinner.

A bare sixty-watt bulb lights the room; Willie's small transistor radio plays low on the floor in the corner, low enough not to be heard anywhere outside the room. His gym towel is stuffed in the crack between the bottom of the door and the floor; absolutely no light escapes. On his lap sits an open notebook: "Dear Mom and Dad." So far, that's it.

He doesn't know if he can't write the letter because he's nervous about being here—waiting without backup to have his head kicked in by an infant Chinese gang—or because he just can't think of what to say to his parents. Many times over this past year he's tried to write them, but each time he gets about this far and jams up. He doesn't know whether to talk about his own guilt for leaving without a trace or about how awful his life became with them after the accident. He wants to be honest but not unnecessarily hurtful. Above all, he wants to repair things. Sometimes he thinks it would be easier to write Johnny first because Johnny would understand better than anyone; but his parents would feel betrayed if he contacted anyone but them.

A *bump* out in the large basement room startles him and he silently lays the notebook on the floor, flips off the radio and jerks the chain on the light bulb to leave the room pitch black. He lies quietly, listening, not sure; maybe it was just the old building settling. He hears it again—still not clearly an unnatural sound, but he reaches down beside the couch and grips his cane, silently turning to put his feet on the floor, then rising to make his way to the door through the darkness. He touches the knob, holding his breath, straining to hear; mentally forcing his heart back down where it belongs. Nothing. He twists the knob, pulling the door open just a crack, then farther, with only the whisper of the towel scooting along the floor to break the dead silence of the building. Dim light shines in through the windows running along the top of the far wall, but the basement walls are dark and seem to swallow it up. Willie can see nothing; he feels watched. Moving along the wall toward the stairway, ears ringing from the fevered pitch of anticipation, he holds the cane lightly in his right hand, fingering the tip like a security blanket; ready in a second to blast some bad guy's head over the center-field bleachers.

He hears the sound again, over by the far wall, still too soft to make out.

"Hawk?" he whispers.

No answer.

"That you, Hawk?"

Still nothing.

He squats quietly on the bottom step, still straining to hear, but only the pounding of his heart comes through. For what seems like an hour he crouches in silence, hearing only dead air from the other side of the room. Finally he stands, waits, and moves carefully back across the floor to the door of the smaller room, sliding inside. He closes it carefully, without a sound, and crouches to replace the towel in the crack. With his ear against the door, he stands a full two minutes in darkness, listening. Finally convinced the monster in the darkness is only a figment of his imagination, he pulls the chain on the light.

Choosing to leave the radio off so he can hear, Willie returns to the notebook; the letter home. He'd almost rather face Kam. Even with all that happened—the night in the racquetball court, the overheard conversation in his parents' bedroom—part of him feels as if *he* betrayed *them.* He wants to apologize; *beg* them to give him another chance; but remembers André's words when he initially brought up the idea of making contact. *Don't go back with your tail between your legs. Like it or not, parents have a contract to stick with their kids through bad times as well as good; your dad didn't do that. That's his responsibility, not yours.*

Willie thinks of the anger and humiliation he sometimes feels when he remembers overhearing his dad virtually wishing Willie had died in the accident. He just doesn't know where to start; which emotions to express; and he stares at the heading. A bang outside the room brings him up with a start. This time he *knows* it's real; farther off in the building somewhere, probably upstairs. He kills the light and again steals out into the larger room, hoping to hear Hawk, or Kato, or *someone* familiar calling his name. Nothing. He moves quickly to the stairs and feels his way along the railing to the upstairs hall, silently thanking Sammy for teaching him to move undetected. There is whispering at the other end of the hall, but he can't make it out; doesn't know if it's friend or foe. He moves behind a set of lockers and listens, then, feeling exposed, retraces his steps downstairs. If it's Hawk, he knows where the room is and he'll find Willie there. If it's the Jo Boys, the room is the best place to hide; without knowing about it, they'd never find him there.

Closing the door behind him once again, he sits on the couch in the darkness and waits. *Where the hell is Hawk? Those guys should have been here hours ago.*

The noises become bolder and Willie is convinced that if it were Hawk and Kato they'd have come down to let him know they were here. They weren't coming to play, to scare him; they know this stuff is serious. The distant bumps and whispers turn to bangs and loud voices, and Willie can only hope that Hawk and Kato will get there soon.

A rap on the door startles his heart straight up into his throat. He holds his breath, frozen.

"Cane Boy." The voice is Kam's. "Come on out, Cane Boy. I know you're in there. I saw you creeping around the basement. Jo Boys see in the dark."

Willie doesn't move; doesn't breathe.

"Time to come on out here, Cane Boy. Jo Boys got business with you."

Willie stands silently, steps back from the door and cocks his cane like a baseball bat. If Kam opens the door, he'll let him step through, then blast his head off the left-field wall.

The rapping comes again; even, patient. The voice is less patient. "Come out."

Willie pictures how he thinks things will look if the door comes open. *Some* light is coming in through the upper windows of the basement, and he's been sitting here in the dark long enough that his eyes should be adjusted, though he doesn't know that for sure, because he can see absolutely nothing in this room. He checks it out by moving the towel away from the crack with his foot. A dim light leaks in. The door will swing away from where he's standing, so if Kam is in the doorway, Willie should be able to see him. He knows he won't have much time; if Kam gets a shot at him with his feet, he's a goner. He positions himself closer to the couch, crouches low, giving what he thinks is his best chance to actually get a silhouette of Kam before Kam sees him.

He waits.

Again the rapping. No voice. Then nothing. Willie's legs begin to cramp in the crouch and he boxes up the pain, corralling it in one place as Sammy taught him; sticks it somewhere in the front of his head a little above the eyes, where he knows he can control it. Several long minutes pass and finally he relaxes just a bit, standing straight to stretch, trying to think what Kam's next move might be. He's not the kind of guy who'll just go away, Willie knows that for sure, and he knows Kam won't be satisfied until he gets even for what Hawk did to him this afternoon; and then some.

Now Willie hears voices again, and the sound of spray cans; then crashing and banging as desks are turned over in classrooms, chalkboards ripped off walls. Fear and anger jockey for the priority position inside him, and he feels helpless standing there in the darkness deciding whether to act or hide. Suddenly he wonders if he could make it to the fire alarm; the noise might scare them. It's down by the stairs and if Kam is still outside the door he wouldn't have a chance, but Willie hasn't heard him in several minutes, and thinks, or wants to think, that Kam is upstairs participating in the destruction. Slowly, with greatest care, he turns the knob; the floor creaks ever so slightly. *Kam. Shifting his weight to put his foot through my skull the second this door opens. He'll wait forever.* Just from what he's learned from Sammy, Willie knows patience has to be foremost in Kam's arsenal of weapons. He lets go of the knob, suddenly wishing he'd waited in the upstairs office where he could have gotten to a phone the second these guys came in. And where the *hell* is Hawk? Willie can't imagine what could have kept him from being here.

In the next instant Willie realizes just how serious this all is; the smell of gasoline burns his nostrils and knots his gut. *Those goddam Jo Boys are going to burn the place down.*

Then the rapping. "Smell that? Best you come out of there, Cane Boy. Things are gonna heat up."

Willie freezes, unable to think. In a flash he sees his new self, everything he's put back together in the last year, go up in smoke. There's no way out of this room except the door. He might be able to wait Kam out, but if he does there's no guarantee he'll get through the basement, up the stairs to the hall and out the front door through the flames. Like a caged animal, he drops into his gut, the way Sammy taught him; places every bit of his energy in his center and trusts it to work things out. He sees the entire main floor of the school. If he can't make it to the front door, there are several classroom windows he can break out. No way in the world Kam can wait out there long enough for fire to block all the escape routes; that would be way too dangerous. He'll wait until he's sure Kam's gone and hope they don't set the fire too close to his door. He moves to the back of the room, waiting. If they do start the fire close to the room, it should burn through quickly. This room is a flimsy afterthought with plywood walls. If they burn through, he'll go out swinging; with the cane, he *might* be as good as Kam. If he gets the chance, Willie thinks, he'll kill Kam.

A loud *whoosh* strains the walls and Willie knows this

is it. He snatches the towel from the crack u der the door, dunks it quickly in the makeshift janitor's sink on the far side of the room before wrapping it around his nose and mouth. The fire is bright under the door, and Willie has no idea whether the whole building is burning or just this area.

The heat quickly becomes nearly intolerable and Willie feels the oxygen being sucked out of the room. He moves to the door, tearing a piece of the towel to cover the knob, turning it very carefully to unlatch it first, then stands back and kicks it open with a crash.

There stands Kam, silhouetted in the flames; crouched in his stance. He's startled momentarily by the flaming door tearing away from its hinges, flying back toward him. Willie is swinging and spinning through the door; aiming the brass ball of the cane for Kam's crotch, then his head. He connects with the former, spins a full 360 degrees on his right leg and brings the cane down on Kam's collarbone before Kam can hit the ground from the first blow. The others are calling to Kam from upstairs; Willie glances to the stairway to see flickering light, telling him the entire school is on fire. In a flash he's across the room, yanking down on the fire alarm, knowing the deafening horn can be heard only there in the building; there is no fire department connection. Smoke burns his eyes and lungs and he drops to his knees to get under it and listen for exactly where the voices are coming from. Stairwells run up from each end of the basement, and he wants to go away from the voices. Satisfied they're coming from the left, he crawls in the other direction. From the stairwell he looks back to see Kam standing, a tight grip on his useless arm, then stumbling; dropping to the floor. His hand reaches out to Willie, and though Willie can't actually hear him, he knows he's calling for help. Kam stands again and Willie decides to leave him, moving quickly on his hands and knees up the stairs. The loud crash of Kam's body again dropping to the floor tells Willie that if he doesn't help, Kam may well burn to death. The voices are silent, Kam's buddies have split. With the towel once again wrapped around his mouth and nose, he works his way back to Kam, clutches him firmly by the collar and begins to drag him backward toward the stairs. He can't see fire now, only smoke, as he pulls him inch by inch to the stairs. Kam screams with each jerk.

At the bottom of the stairs he's exhausted, believing he may suffocate. "Stand up," he says. "I can't drag you up these stairs; you're gonna have to help. If you don't get up, I'll leave you."

Clutching Willie's shoulder, Kam somehow stumbles to the top of the stairs, slipping down twice, coughing and sputtering. At the top he collapses, and Willie drags him down the hall by his injured arm, then out the entrance, where he collapses himself. Tremendous nausea sweeps over him and he pulls himself to his knees to vomit as the fire truck roars through the front gate. The blast of water is the last thing he remembers.

— CHAPTER 20 —

Willie stands on the grass near the edge of the park, watching parents and teachers shaking hands, hugging, talking about how they never thought this or that kid would make it through, congratulating each other on their own perseverance and tenacity. OMLC: One More Last Chance High School. Boy, no kidding. Willing to take any kid, no matter how damaged and angry and beaten down, and give him one more last chance until he finds the one that works or burns out trying. There's André, always André; sometimes gently, sometimes ferociously—always firmly—forcing the acceptance of responsibility, chasing away the fog so life can be seen as it is. André, who just wouldn't stop until OMLC was a place to be proud of—on *his* terms—fixed and painted and painted and fixed, who appeared at five-thirty the morning after the fire—his heart surely broken—to begin again, ripping out burned lumber like a man possessed, declaring a three-week, all-school mini-course in ABR: Advanced Building Restoration. In less than a month OMLC looked better than ever.

Like the old building, its second overhaul in a year complete, Willie feels resurrected. He was a hero for a brief time after the fire, with coverage in the *Tribune;* was even interviewed for a short piece on street gangs in *Oakland Magazine.* Mostly what he said about street gangs was that he would stay away from them if he could. And he did for the rest of the year. The law has Kam cold; sent him to a youth work camp in the Central Valley somewhere, and though very likely other chapters of the Jo Boys continue to wreak havoc around the state, they've not been back.

Lying on the ground outside the burning school, fading in and out of consciousness, Willie had visions of killing Hawk for leaving him there to face the Jo Boys alone, kept thinking he'd never forgive him—never—for leaving him hung out there like that.

Hawk walked into his room at the hospital that night,

his arm wrapped in a cast past the crook of his elbow, and stood, watching, until Willie's eyes opened. Willie squinted, glaring.

"Sorry, man," Hawk said softly. "I was comin', jus' walkin' out the door, an' my brother show, mean on drugs. He dusted; want money, threaten my momma to crack her head, she don't give it. Sister be screamin', I jump between 'em and get throw clean 'cross the kitchen." Hawk shakes his head. "You don't know no dudes meaner than my brother, 'specially when he *up*. I know I got to take him on, he gonna kill somebody. So I do. I get him," he says, pointing to the cast, "but he get me, too. Somebody gonna take him out someday." He looks at Willie; looks sad and guilty. "I get there quick as I can. School be burnin' an' I call; come back quick." He hung his head. "Hawk wouldn't leave you, man . . ."

Willie raised his hand and shook his head and all the animosity left; just dropped away like so much water down the drain. He said, "It's okay, man. You did what you had to. I'd have done the same."

Willie continues to work out with Sammy and Lisa and it is now nearly impossible to tell there was ever anything physically wrong with him if you didn't know him before; hadn't seen him pitch the Crazy Horse Electric game. Tonight he feels almost good enough and strong enough to do it again; but he knows he couldn't. Those days are gone.

Beside him on the court, Hawk and Kato and several other graduates, having shed their tux jackets and spit-shined shoes, play a geared-down version of three-on-three, careful not to work up a sweat, and Willie smiles, admiring Hawk gliding through them in slow motion, dribbling, faking, spinning like a dancer toward the basket, wrapped in his cummerbund and burgundy pants—feet clad in Air Jordans—looking for all the world like Julius Erving opening a line of men's formal wear. He's crazy and he's dangerous, Willie thinks, but he's sure as hell a class act.

Willie hears cheers over by the gate and looks up to see Telephone Man stepping out of his parents' Chevy Nova, head down, sliding around the corner of the gatepost. He wears the same burgundy tux all the boys have, compliments of André, who every year at graduation time works a special deal with Henson's Formal Wear. Willie moves slowly over to intercept Telephone Man, slapping him easily on the back. Jack looks up and smiles sheepishly.

"How 'bout we put these in the office?" Willie asks, pointing to the repair equipment strapped to Jack's hip, giving him an almost eerie Doc Holliday gunslinger look. "Even the most conscientious telephone men take off their gear for high-school graduation."

Jack stares at him blankly for a moment, down at the huge buckle, then back at Willie. "No," he booms, "I don't think so. I feel naked without it."

"Spoken like a true cowboy," Willie says, and drifts back toward the court. He guesses it wouldn't be right for Jack to take off his hardware for the most important event in his life.

The guys finish their makeshift game; Hawk sits on the grass, removing his Air Jordans, as Willie kneels beside him. "You got people coming?" Willie asks.

Hawk nods. "Out the walls. I got uncles and cousins; my daddy might even show. Not many Hawkins' walkin' 'round with a sheepskin. They come out the woodwork to see that."

"Well," Willie says, "just in case things get too crazy

afterward, I just wanna say congratulations and I'm real glad I got to know you."

Hawk slides his foot into his shoe and stops, looks over at Willie, then nods. "Me too, Chief. Didn't know 'bout you when you come here, with you cane an' you funny talk. Thought you might be another Telephone Man. But you my man, Chief. I learn shit watchin' you, won't *never* forget. Jus' sorry I couldn't get here sooner, night of the fire."

"Hey, man, you got the fire department here."

Hawk nods. "Yeah, but ol' Hawk want a piece of that China boy. *You* get him, though, Chief, an' that's about as good. You my man, Crazy Horse."

Willie reaches over to shake his hand, then moves toward the building as André calls everyone inside to the student lounge, which appears transformed for the ceremony, with crepe-paper streamers, a revolving mirrored ball and a huge purple velvet banner reading: CONGRATULATIONS OMLC GRADUATES.

The ceremony is different from a lot of high-school commencement exercises Willie has seen. Only eighteen students will graduate, and while the valedictorian and salutatorian deliver their traditional addresses, so does anyone else who feels inclined to talk out loud about what the night means. Almost everyone does, most simply repeating the truth: simply that, if not for OMLC—if they hadn't received this last chance—they would be in the street.

Willie finds himself wondering what Angel will say; after all, she *is* in the street, but when her name is read, she takes the diploma, looks out at the audience, then over to the graduates and simply says, "Thanks." Willie looks out to see Lacey nodding his head and clapping.

Hawk is introduced as "Doctor Hawk," referring to

Dr. J of the Philadelphia 76ers, and is presented, along with his diploma, with a leather game ball, signed by all the members of the graduating class. "You could go on," André says, handing Hawk the ball. "It'd be tough, but you can if you want."

Hawk thanks everyone—his mother several times—and goes on to say he doesn't know what he'll do now, but he's real glad to have this chance to choose. Then he looks straight out at his dad and says, "I tol' you I ain't no worthless shit," and his dad looks at the ground. Hawk nods and walks proudly back to sit down. Willie can only imagine the history behind that.

When Jack's name is called, he stands, staring at the floor, and pulls his tuxedo jacket tight around him, covering the top half of his telephone gear, takes a deep breath and walks toward André at the podium. André hands Jack his diploma, expecting him to take it and slink on back to his seat, but Telephone Man hesitates.

"Would you like to say something, Jack?"

Telephone Man starts back, stops, then slowly steps up to the podium. He looks out at the small crowd, again starting to turn away, but André says, "Go ahead, Jack, it's okay. This is a big night. Take a chance."

Telephone Man takes a deep breath, clutching the sides of the podium like they could somehow save his life. "I'm really glad I went here," he booms; there is no decibel control on Jack's voice. "It used to be nobody liked me where I went to school, and then I came here and nobody liked me either. But then I got beat up and Hawktor Doctor went and got that Chinese kid and beat him up because he beat me up, and I knew that even though he's tough and acts mean and scares people sometimes, Hawktor Doctor must really like me." Tears start to roll out of Telephone Man's eyes and he

looks straight at Hawk. "And that's the first time anybody really liked me and I'm glad I went here." Jack
doesn't know exactly how to stop, so he bows to the
crowd and walks back to his seat; and Hawk starts the
applause. Hawk has long since quit trying to convince
Telephone Man that it's Doctor Hawk—not Hawktor
Doctor—because Jack doesn't know Dr. J. from Alexan-
der Graham Bell; all he knows is that Hawk's name is
supposed to rhyme and that's as close as he gets.

When Kato's name is called, he launches into a tale of
an old Roman couple who grew the biggest berry in the
entire empire. Hoping for some kind of meaningful
analogy, the crowd listens in pained silence as he tells of
nobility coming from far and near to see this miraculous
berry and of how finally the emperor himself gets word
of its enormity and decides he wants it for himself. But
the couple won't give it up and no amount of negotia-
tion will sway them. "Finally," Kato says, just as André
is about ready to cut him off and save his life, "these old
folks hear a knock at the door an' when the ol' dude
opens it, see he bein' confronted by a whole squad full
of Roman soldiers. But he an old fart and he let 'em in
'cause he think they just wanna see this big-ol'-ass berry.
But then the head soldier put his hand on the old man's
shoulder and he say in his big official voice, 'Uh-uh, old
man, we come to seize your berry, not to praise it.' "
Kato looks up at the audience with a big grin until one
by one they get it and a rolling groan works its way clear
through. When they're finished, he smiles again and
says, "But see, the point be, if I didn't go to school here
an' work my butt off in English class, I wouldn't even
know that be a joke."

André puts his hands on Kato's shoulders and points
him toward his seat, looking out at the audience. "I

don't want to be the one to tell him that's *not* a joke. I'd appreciate it if each of you would mention it in the receiving line."

Willie's name is announced last and there's a long round of applause as he approaches the podium; the audience knows him from the fire and he has special status. André describes him as "Comeback Cowboy of the Year," presenting him with a tacky three-foot-high trophy with that inscription, composed mostly of plastic with a bareback bronc rider on top. Willie thinks that's pretty funny. When the laughter dies, he takes a folded paper from the inside pocket of his rented tux and spreads it out in front of him. He's thought long and hard about what he wants to say tonight, and he's very nervous. He looks out into the audience; at Lacey, decked out in his dress whites, jewelry on every finger and a painted lady on his arm; at Lisa in her slinky two-tone blue dress that turns her smooth skin to polished mahogany; and Sammy beside her, his inch-long hair shooting out of his head like some kind of electric surprise; then over at André, who stands to the side watching, smiling, somehow knowing exactly how Willie feels.

Willie forces a lump back down his throat. "This school," he says, "saved my life. I don't mean it made me a better person, or picked me up when I was really down, or taught me the true meaning of anything. I mean it saved my life; because when I came here I was to the end of me. My family was wrecked and I thought I'd wrecked it. My brain didn't work right and the physical skills I had always depended on were shot completely to Hell." He looks out to Lacey. "My friend Mr. Casteel picked me up off the street and gave me a home; his home. I have to admit I haven't always been the perfect roommate, and I would have to say our lifestyles are somewhat different, but old Lacey's stuck with me, and in his way he's a wise man, and I owe him a lot."

Lacey looks around the crowd, smiling, a bit embarrassed.

Willie goes on. "Nobody here preached at me. Nobody told me everything would be okay, or that I should go back home to my parents and work things out when I knew the time for that wasn't here yet. They let me figure it out for myself; *demanded* that I figure it out for myself; but they never deserted me. And now, I'm ready to go back home. I don't know what will happen there; whether I can stay and make it or not, but at least I'm strong enough to give it a try." He pauses, looking at his notes, then folds them, placing them in his pocket, and looks back out at the crowd, at Lacey.

"I know how lucky I am," he says. "My parents were always there for me, but then the really hard times came and they couldn't do it, and I chased my friends away and then there was nobody. And my parents are good people, really they are; so are my friends. So I really do know how lucky I am that when things were at their worst, out pops André, and Lisa, and this magic school."

He sips water from the glass on the podium and clears his throat. "See, I'm not a tough guy; Lacey Casteel can tell you that. And I'm real aware that if most of you had known me back before, when I lived in Montana, you might very well have hated my guts. Because I had everything; and I had people there to protect me and make sure I didn't lose it. And there are lots of people like that; people whose lives are protected from the day they're born until the day they die. But no matter how wonderful those lives seem, if they're not contested, never put up against the wall, then they exist inside very narrow walls, and because of that I believe they lose value, in the most basic sense of the word. I guess what I'm saying is that my life is more valuable because I got knocked out of my favored spot. I can't believe I'm saying that, but I am and I know it's true. I learned it from the people who picked me up here."

Willie takes a deep breath and looks around; at Angel, who stares past him; at Hawk, who meets his stare and lets him in; at Lisa, who radiates her integrity right back at him. He looks at Lacey, who can't hold his gaze, then back at Sammy, who just looks *charged;* gleeful and charged. "A few more minutes and I'll get off it," he says, dropping his gaze to the podium. "There's a man in the audience tonight who comes from somewhere else. I mean, I'm pretty sure there's a spaceship parked in the near vicinity waiting to beam him right up. When I first met him, I thought he was one of those Japanese guys who got lost on a Pacific island during World War II and nobody bothered to tell him when it was over." Willie looks again at Sammy, who is grinning from ear to ear. "But then he talked to me, mostly without words, and I think he told me a whole lot of what I'm going to need to be an adult. He showed me how my mind and body are just different parts of the same thing and that there are no limits for either; that most of the really important answers are already inside me and I don't have to go outside looking for them. He taught me how to go to my gut to survive.

"I asked him once what he believed in. He was up on the roof here at school, hanging down over the edge painting the underside of the rain gutters, and he stopped painting and looked at me and flipped paint on me and said he believes in lust and passion and good old common sense. And in staying alive."

Willie shrugs. "I probably don't even know what half of that means, but I sure like it and I'm going to find out." He thanks everyone again for listening to him carry on, picks up his trophy by the comeback cowboy's neck and walks back to his chair.

"I beat that guy one-on-one. Do or die. Make it, take it," Telephone Man booms to nobody in particular.

Willie sits down; Hawk leans over and whispers, "Whooee, Chief be sayin' some *words* up there. Don' be givin' you too much more play, you be runnin' for some *office.*"

— CHAPTER 21 —

Willie boards the Greyhound at 8:30 a.m., turns and waves once again to Lacey, decked out in his AC Transit uniform, looking for all the world like an honest man making an honest living. "This don't work out," Lacey says one more time, "you take that ticket Lacey give you an' head right back down here."

Willie smiles. "I will, Lacey, really I will. I know I have a home here." He steps back off the bus for a moment and walks toward Lacey, who looks bewildered at his approach. "If it means anything," Willie says, "you're one and one now. You broke one and you fixed one."

Lacey looks him in the eye and nods, leaving his thoughts where they are.

Willie slaps him on the shoulder and steps back onto the bus.

He could have flown. He has money of his own saved now, since Lacey started paying him for extra work and André did, too; and anyway, Lacey offered to buy the ticket. But Willie needs the cushion of space and time to ease him back to Coho. He wants to return through the same tunnel that brought him here, as if retracing his steps will help him find the clues to tell him how to be back. Willie knows he should have called; should call now, for that matter; but he just can't imagine what he would say over the phone. He knows it isn't right to show up without any warning, but he's doing this the best way he can and it will just have to do.

He chooses a window seat behind the driver, stuffing his pack under the seat, having checked most of his luggage earlier at the desk. He hopes to sleep; he was up most of last night with the rest of his graduating class before finally collapsing for a few hours, possibly for the last time, on the makeshift bed in Lacey's living room. But sleep never came; his mind racing randomly from the night at the fishing hole with Jenny to discovering her lie in the breezeway, to the Crazy Horse Electric game, to the night he crouched outside his parents' bedroom only to discover what an immense burden he had become. He used every trick Sammy or Lisa ever taught him to quiet his mind, but it was off and running on its own and all he could do was go with it until finally it was time to get up and gather his things and ride to the bus terminal with Lacey.

Willie's heart leaps as the big diesel engine cranks up; the driver moves among the passengers, leaving the engine running, checking tickets and rearranging some of the carry-on luggage. As the bus pulls out of the garage, Willie watches Lacey standing, arms folded, looking powerful and confident, without a trace of the horror in his life, and Willie marvels at the astonishing ability of human beings to go on. He waves; Lacey waves back and doesn't move from his spot until the bus is out of sight.

Winding through the city streets toward the freeway, Willie notices how different they look to him now, in the light of day and a year and a half later, from how they looked that first night when they stole from him, through terror, what little dignity he had left. Perspectives.

The Greyhound rolls over the coastal hills out into the Central Valley, already intolerably hot in mid-June, and Willie drifts in and out of consciousness, the singing of the wheels finally allowing his mind to rest. In a daze, he watches the Sierra roll by, the bus stopping at every town of even the slightest consequence, gently bumping him awake, then easing him back to sleep. In the darkness he wakes to find they are in the high Nevada desert, headed north toward Oregon, then Idaho. Though the sign tells him not to talk to the "Operator," the bus driver sees him awake in the mirror and strikes up a rambling conversation in which the most significant thing Willie learns is that the occasional bumping sound he hears is the result of legions of jackrabbits crossing the street without looking both ways. The driver calls this stretch between Winnemucca and the Oregon border "The Trail of Entrails."

By morning Willie feels rested and almost impatient to be in Coho, though there are several hours of travel left. He's ready to face what he left.

* * *

A little after four in the afternoon, Willie stands beside his luggage on the sidewalk outside Carson's drugstore, looking up and down the main street of Coho. He saw Mr. Carson through the window when he got off the bus, but there was no glimmer of recognition on his face, so he didn't go in. He looks up and down the street once more, then steps into the doorway. "Okay if I leave this stuff here for a little while?" he asks, pointing to his two suitcases.

Mr. Carson says, "Sure," without even looking up and Willie slides them around the corner out of the way, hoisting his pack up over one shoulder as he begins the seven-block walk to his house. He passes lots of familiar faces on the way, but receives nothing more than a friendly smile. A block from his house he stops, gathering his courage, trying to visualize what his mother will do when she sees him standing there. He wonders again for a moment if the boy in the Portland terminal ever mailed the cards, but knows it doesn't really matter. For a moment he considers walking back to the drugstore to call ahead, but takes a deep breath instead, centers himself and moves on. A half-block away, he sees a strange car parked in the driveway and he slows down to think, then walks onto the front lawn. He stops, staring at a two-foot hand-carved sign over the porch proclaiming his parents' house to be THE MILLERS. He stands, staring, a vague, undefined fear carving deeper into the already empty pit of his stomach. He's way off balance and for a moment can't think what to do next. He could go to the door and ask, but somehow he can't bear the thought of a stranger confirming any of his worst fears. Willie doesn't know any Millers.

He turns slowly to walk back toward town, thinking

his next move will come to him on the way, feeling somehow foolish, and wanting to get away; to not be seen in his old neighborhood looking bewildered.

Stepping into the phone booth outside the drugstore, he searches his pockets for a quarter; finds nothing. He curses to himself and walks into the store, placing a dollar on the counter for a pack of gum he doesn't want. Mr. Carson looks right at him, seeing a stranger, hands him his change absently, telling him to have a good day. Willie says, "You, too," and heads back out to the booth, where he flips through the R's, looking for Johnny's number.

"Hello?"

"Yes. Is Johnny Rivers there?"

"I don't think so. Let me check." Silence, then, "No, I don't think so. I think he's at work. Can I take a message?"

"No, that's okay," Willie says. "Could you tell me where he works?"

The other end is quiet for a second and Willie knows Johnny's mom must think she recognizes the voice. "Down at Wilkie's Conoco. Who is this?"

"It's nobody. Thanks. I'll try to catch him down there."

"Wait . . ." But Willie hangs up.

Wilkie's is just three blocks up Main Street from the drugstore and Willie sits on the curb beside the phone booth looking at the sign, absently fondling his cane, then pushes himself up, heading toward it. Time to blow his cover.

Willie stands in the doorway to the front office of Wilkie's Conoco while Johnny counts out change for

Mrs. O'Conners, and steps aside as she thanks him and moves past Willie toward her car.

"Johnny?"

Johnny looks up, stands staring, wiping his hands with his grease rag, his brain running through the fund of information telling him this can't be Willie Weaver but it sure as hell is but it doesn't look exactly like him but it does.

"Willie? Willie Goddam Weaver? Jesus, are you kidding me? Willie Weaver?"

Willie tosses Johnny the cane.

Johnny stares at the brass baseball in absolute disbelief, then back at Willie. He says, "Shit," and looks again at the cane.

"How you doin'?"

"I don't know," Johnny says. "Jesus, where you been? I thought . . ."

"It's a long story," Willie says. "I'll tell you later. Do you know what happened to my parents? I was over at the house and it's sold." He watches Johnny's face fall momentarily as the bell signals a customer on the island.

"Lemme get this," Johnny says. "I'll be right back." He trots out onto the island, watching Willie through the front window as he pumps ten gallons of regular into the tank of a brown '76 Datsun, washes the windshield and collects the money.

"I probably know where your dad is," Johnny says, pulling a bottle of pop from the machine outside the office. "Want one?"

Willie nods. "Sure. Orange."

"I don't know how to tell you this," Johnny says, handing him the pop, hesitating. "Your mom and dad sort of fell apart. I mean . . ."

"It's okay, Johnny. Just go ahead and tell me. All the stuff that's gone on in the last year and a half, I can take it. Just tell me. Where's my mom and dad?"

"Well, your dad's probably over at Dinghy's." Johnny grimaces, waits.

"Dinghy's? What's he doing at Dinghy's?"

"He's there a lot, Willie. Your dad's been drunk a lot since you left. A lot of people are really worried about him. Nobody can do anything, though, 'cause he's getting pretty mean."

"My dad?"

Johnny just breathes deep and raises his eyebrows.

"What about Mom?"

Johnny takes another deep breath. "She got married."

"She got married! My folks are split? They're divorced?"

"Things have been bad, Willie. After you left, your folks started fighting really bad. Cops got called twice and your dad spent the night in jail. Pretty soon they were just split and your dad moved into the Ranch Motel and nobody saw your mom for a while. Then she started seeing this guy named Don Boudreaux—he owns a bunch of those condos over at Badger Lake—and pretty soon your house was up for sale and your mom was getting married. Everybody thinks you're dead."

Willie's in shock. This is worse than his worst fear.

"Look at this," Johnny says, pointing to the counter below the oil display. A half-gallon milk carton displays a likeness of Willie on the side, taken from his sophomore class picture. It says: MISSING. There is a description, with his age and location at the time of disappearance. Willie's heart sinks. He knows the kid in the

Portland bus terminal never mailed the postcards, and he wishes he had made some other effort to let *someone* know he had stayed alive. His need to stay hidden for the last year and a half suddenly seems selfish and stupid. "Look," he says, "I'll see you later. I'm going over to Dinghy's and see if my dad's there. You know where my mom lives?"

"They live in one of the condos over at Badger. I'll drive you over there after work if you want. Listen, you can stay at our place. My mom and dad would love to have you."

"Maybe," Willie says. "I'll see, okay? Thanks, Johnny, really."

"Yeah. Hey, man, I'm really sorry . . ."

Willie nods and heads down the street toward Dinghy's tavern.

The lights are low and Willie squints to adjust his eyes as he walks through the door. On the far side of the room a man and a woman shoot a game of eight-ball, and an old man rests his head on a table near the bar, seemingly passed out. Behind the bar a young guy Willie doesn't recognize runs a wet rag over the bar top, absently lip-synching the Hank Williams Jr. tune playing low on the jukebox. He looks up as Willie enters. "Can I help you?"

Willie saw his dad's Bronco out on the street and knows he's around somewhere. As his eyes adjust better, he spots him down at the end of the bar, nursing a draft beer, reading the *Helena Times.* Big Will doesn't look up. "I need to talk to him," Willie says, nodding toward his dad.

"Can't serve you without ID."

"No ID," Willie says. "I just want to talk to that guy. He's my dad."

The bartender looks surprised. "You Willie?"

Willie nods and walks down the bar to the stool beside his dad, who hasn't even looked up from his paper. He sits. "Dad?"

Big Will looks up, his eyes watery and bloodshot. He looks older than he did, vacant. Willie can't believe the emptiness, the despair written on his face. Their eyes meet and Willie holds his gaze. Big Will is confused, glances back to his paper, then again to Willie. "Get out of here," he says. "You get out of here."

"Dad, it's me, Willie."

"I know who the hell you are. Get out of here."

"No."

"I'll kick your ass," Big Will says.

Willie didn't expect this. It doesn't match any of the hundreds of scenarios that ran through his head on the long bus trip back. And he's not going to accept it. He feels a surge of power; anger. "You might try," he says. "You don't look up to it."

Big Will whirls on his stool to face Willie straight on. "You little shit," he says. "You little shit. You run away without a word and leave us here to let our lives fall apart. Then you walk in here over a year later saying 'Dad?'" He mimics the last word, spits it out like a turd under his curled lip, his voice whiny. Willie wants to slug him.

"Well," Big Will says, "your mom and I aren't married anymore and I'm not your dad." He turns back to his paper and his beer.

Willie's stunned. He doesn't want to leave without talking, but has no idea what to say, so he just nods slowly and rises to go. "I'll be back, Dad. Or I'll catch

you over at your place. But we're going to talk, you and
me, whether you like it or not." Then he's out the door.
His gut aches and burns; his heart, like an African drum,
beats out a desperate message he can't understand.
Pain and rage swell in him until he thinks he'll burst,
but there's nothing to do but sit on the curb and take
deep breaths until it feels under control.

"You got wheels?" Willie asks Johnny as he marks his
time on the time sheet, ready to leave work.

"I got a car now, why?"

"I need something to get over to see my mom if she's
at Badger Lake."

"You know how to ride your dad's bike?"

"Sure," Willie says. "He taught me when he first
bought it. Why? Is it still around?"

"Yeah," Johnny says. "It's over at our place. We're
selling it for him. My dad just overhauled it and put it
out front."

Willie's mind involuntarily drifts back to the times
behind his dad on the Shadow, pushing against the se-
cure edges of their world, knowing they were safe just
because Big Will was in control. He can't believe the
man on the bike and the man in the bar are the same.
Tears well up, but he fights them back. He won't fold.

Johnny throws his grease rag into a bucket under the
counter and hollers to Mr. Jackson in the back office that
he's out of there and they trot over to a perfectly recon-
ditioned red-and-white '57 Chevy in the side parking
lot. "What do you think?" Johnny says, shoving his key
into the trunk lock to reveal a cooler. He pulls out two
cans of ice-cold beer and flips one to Willie. "Graduation party last night," he says. "Leftovers."

Without consideration, Willie pops the top on the beer and puts it to his mouth. He hasn't had a taste of alcohol since the night at Johnny's party when the ground dropped out from under him. It tastes good.

"Why don't you go over to Badger in the morning?" Johnny says after hearing Willie's rendition of the events in Dinghy's. "Give yourself some time to think. God, I can't believe how you look. I thought you were crippled for good." He pulls against the curb in front of the drugstore and Willie jumps out to get his luggage. Johnny moves the cooler over and they stuff both suitcases into the trunk. "My folks would love to have you stay."

Willie agrees. He needs time. Johnny is the best person to be with for that. He can catch up and he can think.

Johnny's in the living room calling some of the old gang to come over for a surprise, and initially Willie considers stopping him, but lets it go. Whatever's going to happen is going to happen and it might as well be now.

". . . and come by yourself," Johnny is saying. Willie knows he's talking to Jenny, a subject they've avoided until now.

He sits on the couch as Johnny hangs up. "She still with Rhodes?" he asks.

"Naw," Johnny said. "Not really with anyone. I think she felt really guilty after you left. She's stayed pretty much to herself. Had a great year in basketball, though. She's almost as good an athlete as you. Or as you were. Or whatever."

Jenny is the last to arrive and by then most everyone

is over the shock and just pumping Willie for details about his life and catching him up. The doorbell rings and Johnny hollers, "Come in." His parents have escaped for the evening.

Jenny walks in through the kitchen, depositing a sack of chips and dip and chocolate-covered peanuts on the counter, and steps into the living room. "So what's the surprise, Johnny?"

"Just having a little party," Johnny says, looking up from the couch beside Willie.

Jenny doesn't see Willie; doesn't recognize him. "So what's surprising about that? The surprise would be if you *weren't* having a party."

Willie says, "Hi, Jen," and she freezes, her entire muscular structure going slack. She puts her hand on the back of a chair for support. He says, "How you doing?"

In that instant Jenny's eyes go hard. "You son of a bitch," she says.

"You should go have a beer with my dad."

"You son of a bitch," she says again, her hair flying as she whirls to run from the room.

"Jen, wait," Willie says, but she's gone.

Johnny runs after her, catching her at her car while Willie closes his eyes; drops his head back into the pillow on the couch; waiting. In seconds Johnny appears in the doorway alone. "Too much surprise," he says. "She'll be okay. She'll get over it."

The party runs awhile longer, but the heart's out of it and people begin drifting away early. Only Petey tries to keep it going; tries to relive the old days and the Crazy Horse Electric game. Only Petey has the will to make everything go back; and if left to his own devices, he could do it.

Willie and Johnny stand at the door as their friends file out, telling Willie they're glad he's back and they hope things work out for him with Jenny and with his family and everything; giving him bits of encouragement. But Willie feels so apart from all this. The fact is that two of the four people he loved the most when his life was real here seem to hate his guts, and the jury's still out on his mother. Only Johnny hung in for him. That's not enough. He's sinking.

"You know where the key to my dad's bike is?" he asks and Johnny gets it from the mantel. "I'm going for a little ride, like for a half-hour or so. Don't go to bed yet, okay?"

Johnny agrees and Willie slips through the hall door to the garage, where he takes the FOR SALE sign off the windshield of the Shadow and lays it on the workbench. He backs it out onto the concrete driveway and hits the starter button, hearing the engine roar to life like it always did. Cutting a tight turn in the driveway, he moves easily, carefully, through the neighborhood. Though he knows how to ride, he's not Big Will and the bike is plenty big enough to scare him. He heads slowly out of town, away from the bluffs; away from where he and his dad used to ride.

The night is warm and his confidence builds as the lights of Coho fade behind him; he pushes the Shadow up to seventy, then backs off, remembering what speed can do at just the wrong time and place. *I've lost all I can afford to lose*—his mother's voice, at the lake before the accident. Willie can't believe there's this much sadness in the world, when a guy is just doing all he can do to get by. He looks up at the stars and at the quartermoon gently bathing the highway in grayish blue, and turns up the speed. What the hell.

* * *

"You *call* your mother first," Mrs. Rivers says to Willie at breakfast. "If Johnny just showed up after more than a year without warning me first, why, I'd snatch him bald-headed."

"She would, too," Johnny says, his mouth full of corn flakes. "She snatches me bald-headed for *not* being gone more than a year."

Mrs. Rivers ignores him. "You call, Willie. Or I will."

Willie nods. He's tried surprising people and so far that hasn't worked to his advantage. "I'll call her."

When he does call, a man answers, telling him his mother's not home but that she should be within the next half-hour or so. Willie identifies himself and after a short silence the voice on the other end says, "Well, come on over here. And you hurry up. Your mom will be thrilled." A pause. "She's married now, you know . . ."

"I know," Willie says. "You must be Don."

"Yes. Yes, I am. And I'm anxious to meet you, Willie, so hurry on over. Have you got transportation? I could come get you . . ."

"No, I've got transportation," Willie says. "Thanks anyway."

The day is hot, but Willie goes into the garage to get his old helmet, meant to be sold with the bike, because he never wants his mom to see him without one again, never wants to scare her, or keep anything from her. On the outside of town, he stops to remove his shirt, and momentarily thinks of strapping the helmet to the sissy bar until he gets close, but that's just like the old days and he keeps it on.

Though it's a two-lane highway to Badger, traffic is

light and the twenty-mile trip is quick. He may wear his helmet, but Willie Weaver still likes speed.

Willie and his mom walk along the man-made beach in front of the condominiums that she and her husband Don now own. Don was cordial, easy to talk to, though Willie couldn't shake that almost otherworldly feeling in the pit of his stomach, seeing this man who is his mother's husband now, thinking of them kissing and close; intimate; and he had to keep forcing his head movies out. Finally, he just asked his mom if she'd go for a walk.

"You fish?" he asks. Badger is one of the better rainbow-trout lakes around.

"Some. Not like I used to. Why?"

"I don't know," Willie says. "Just wondered, I guess. Just looking for some connection to the old days." He's put it off for more than an hour, and finally he asks. "What happened? With you and Dad, I mean."

"Oh, Willie, it was so bad. I got crazy. Your dad got mean, started drinking. We were sure you were dead, and we each saw all the ways we'd killed you. We blamed ourselves, we blamed each other. There was so much confusion; so much anger. Everything that was swept under the rug when Missy died came out, and pretty soon I was taking cruel shots at your dad that reduced him to nothing and he was beating me up." Sandy shakes her head, absently kicking sand into the water. "Then I ran away. There was nothing left."

Willie stares into the water, then over at his mom. "I couldn't stay," he says. "I *would* have died. I'm sorry I didn't contact you; I still don't know for sure why I didn't, probably because I thought you would have talked me back before I was ready. All I know is I did what I could. And it saved me."

Sandy nods. "I know. You can't blame yourself. Your father and I were supposed to be the adults."

"Still, you couldn't have expected . . ."

"No, but you don't always get what you expect. I wish someone, sometime when I was growing up, would have told me what expectations would get me. I wasn't ready for any of this, Willie, and neither was your father. The most significant thing that happened to him in all the time before we were married was a stupid football game named after a bowl of flowers. And to tell the truth, I thought it was as important as he did." Sandy shakes her head and they begin walking again. "Our parents, schools, everyone tells us things will be a certain way when we're adults and if they're not that way, we should make them be; or at least pretend. But after a certain point that just doesn't work."

"Yeah," Willie says. "I know."

"You know, we went to see your counselor after you left. Mr. Wheat. He laid it out for us—said not many families survive one death, let alone two. He was helpful, but your dad got angry, called him a wimp and quit going. It didn't do a lot of good for me to go alone; in fact, it just caused more trouble."

"So what about Don?"

Sandy smiles a sad smile. "Well, I don't love him like I loved your dad once, but we might only get one chance like that in a lifetime. Who knows? But he's a good man and he pulled me out when all there was for me was despair. If it hadn't been for him, I'd probably be at the other end of the bar in Dinghy's competing with your dad to see who gets liver disease first." She puts her hand on Willie's head. "Give Don a chance. You don't have to make him your dad. Just know he's my friend."

Willie agrees to stay for dinner, where he meets his four-year-old stepsister, who is with Don for the week. Her name is Molly. She is afraid of Willie and stays very close to her father's leg when Willie talks to her.

"You're welcome to stay as long as you want," Don says over dessert. "I don't know your plans, but I could get you work over the summer if you want."

Willie thanks him politely and says he thinks he'll stay with Johnny, for a few days at least, to think. He's irritated at himself that he judges this man by the fact that he wears dress socks with his Bermuda shorts while doing lawn work; that he wants Don to be cool if he's going to be his mother's husband, though he fully trusts his mother's judgment that Don is a decent man. You feel what you feel, as Sammy says.

Willie pulls into Coho, deciding to take a run past the Ranch Motel on the off chance his dad is there. The tiny kidney-shaped pool in the yard is cracked and filled with leaves and other winter sludge, and wild shrubbery grows out onto the parking lot. Big Will's Bronco is parked in front of Cabin 3 and Willie pulls the bike up beside it. After three knocks the door opens and there stands Big Will, just awakened, his eyes so bloodshot from alcohol and sleep that he looks to Willie like a special effect. Willie takes a deep breath. "Why don't you let me come in?" he says.

Big Will stares evenly, then relaxes a little. "Because I don't want you to see," he says. "Wait out here and I'll get my shoes on."

Willie leans against the Bronco hood for less than a minute before his dad appears in the doorway again, saying, "Let's get some coffee. I been thinking. You're right, we should talk." He notices the Shadow. "Found the bike, huh? You can have it if you want. I don't dare ride it anymore; I found a slower way to kill myself."

They walk across the street to Jackie's Home Cookin' and order up a "bottomless pot of coffee" and two orders of Big Will's "usual."

"Guess you never thought you'd see your old man come to this, huh?" Big Will says, breaking a long silence.

"Guess not," Willie says. Then, "God, Dad, what're we gonna do?"

"I don't know. I spent all that time teaching you to be responsible and for the life of me I can't remember why. I just can't make myself care anymore, Willie. I'd quit drinking—I really could—but it feels too shitty to be sober. I always played it so goddam tough, but I don't think I can make it without your mother. And even if she weren't with Don, I couldn't make it *with* her now; not after the way I treated her. I don't want to sound melodramatic, but I'm just waiting it out."

"She said it got bad."

Big Will nods. "A mistress of the understatement. It got *terrible.*" He takes another deep breath. "I've been thinking since I yelled at you in the bar. I wanted to apologize, try to work something out with you. I'm apologizing, but I don't think I can work anything out right now. I mean, you can't stay with me or anything. I'm barely keeping alive."

Inside, Willie's heart is broken, but he doesn't show—takes himself away like Sammy taught him—because he doesn't want to make things worse. "I understand that," he says. "Is there anything I can do? Anything you need from me?"

Big Will shakes his head.

Willie reaches into his pocket and pulls out a sealed, crumpled envelope that Lacey gave him just before he got on the bus. "Don' you go readin' this," Lacey had said. "Jus' give it to you daddy."

"Guy I stayed with in Oakland wanted me to deliver this to you," Willie said. "I haven't read it."

Big Will opens the envelope, reads the short note with no visible reaction and lays it in front of Willie. "Black guy, huh?"

Willie nods. "Yeah." He reads the note:

Dear Mr. Will Weaver
Here you boy back. He fix. Be careful how you treet him, he special. If you don't want him, send him back.
                                   Sinserly,
                                   Lacey Casteel

Willie smiles at the thought of Lacey composing the letter exactly the way he talks, leaving out all the emotion, writing tough and to the point.

They talk awhile longer; Willie tells how he got himself back together physically and his dad seems interested, even mildly impressed. He tells Willie he did a hell of a job. After they eat, Willie walks his dad back to the motel and says he'll see him again.

He calls Johnny's house to let them know where he is and that he's already had dinner, so not to hold anything for him. Then he rides the bike over to Jenny's. Might as well get it all out of the way today.

Jenny's mom welcomes him with a big hug and tells him how the whole town is so glad he's okay and that he looks good, much better than anyone would have expected, and offers him three kinds of dessert. Willie respectfully declines and asks Jenny if she'll go for a walk with him.

On the street, he apologizes again for not contacting anyone, but holds his ground: he just couldn't.

"Do you know what I've been through this last year and a half?" Jenny asks. "Thinking I drove you out; that I killed you?"

"It must've been bad."

"Yeah," she says sarcastically. "It must've been. Willie, why couldn't you have just called? Sent a card? Anything."

He starts to explain his one feeble attempt in the Portland terminal, but stops. "Look, Jen, I didn't, okay? There's nothing I can do about that now. I'm not going to spend our time together answering questions that don't have answers. You guys act like you're the only ones that got hurt in all this; like I've been holed up in some California country club laughing at the great joke I played. Everybody's hurt, okay? Now we can either find a way to bury it and go from here or we can leave it like it is. Either way, at least you know I'm not dead, so you couldn't have killed me."

He tries to force the anger down, but it's like an anvil on his chest. He closes his eyes, like Sammy taught him, and forces the anvil up; he softens. "Look, you should be happy. There's no more guilt. I'm okay, maybe better than ever. You did what you had to do and so did I. Hell, I knew you'd have to start seeing someone else; I was a *troll.* I just needed you to be honest about it and there was no way you could. If it had been reversed, I'd have done the same thing you did."

Jenny stops in the middle of the sidewalk. The evening sun shines off her face and lights her hair and Willie remembers how much he loved her once. "Willie, I can't talk about this now. I'm too hurt and too angry and too confused. I don't even know how I feel. If I talked now, it would just be gibberish and I wouldn't mean what I say."

Early Sunday morning Willie straps all his belongings to the back of the Shadow and says goodbye to Johnny Rivers. It isn't time. He loves Montana. He loves the freedom, the wilderness; but he feels crippled here; like he did before he left. They all know where to find him, he left the address of OMLC. He and Johnny hug, promise to meet. He's let everyone know he'll be back.

He rides the bike slowly to his old house, walks up to the door and knocks. A woman, who must be Mrs. Miller, answers the door in her robe. She has been cooking breakfast for her family.

"Excuse me," he says, "I'm really sorry to bother you, but my name's Willie Weaver and my sister died in this house a long time ago. I wonder if you could just let me see her room. I'm leaving."

The woman doesn't question him, only stands aside, saying, "Of course," looking to her husband reading the morning paper in his easy chair, lifting a finger to her lips at him.

Willie walks through the living room and stands in the doorway to what was Missy's room when he was twelve. There's a crib there, and a baby; a beautiful, round baby with most of its fist crammed into its mouth, breathing easily, like Missy wasn't the day she died. He walks over and puts his hand softly on the baby's head, then down on its open hand. The baby instinctively squeezes his finger and Willie cries.

"Her name's Melinda." Mrs. Miller's soft voice comes from behind him, and Willie says, "Melinda," without turning around. He takes a deep breath, fighting to hold the tears until he can get outside. "She's beautiful," he says. "Thank you."

Outside, he gets on the Shadow and without looking back heads south for Oakland.